**Dylan didn't question her, though.
He merely headed for the shop door.**

"Four-thirty tomorrow," he repeated. "Text me your address and I'll bring a car with no dents and more than two seats."

That confused her, too. But she felt so dazed by then that she thought it might have been perfectly clear to someone else.

She only nodded and watched him open the door.

As he went through it he cast her one last glance over his shoulder. He had the kind of smile on his face that said he liked what he saw when he caught that final sight of her. Then he pulled the door closed after himself and he was gone.

And that was when Abby deflated. Swallowed hard. And wondered if she'd stepped into some other world or something.

Because somehow she didn't feel as though she was still in her own.

* * *

**THE CAMDENS OF COLORADO:
They've made a fortune in business.
Can they make it in the game of love?**

Dear Reader,

Abby Crane and Dylan Camden are from two different worlds. Dylan was raised a child of privilege. Abandoned at two years old, Abby grew up in foster care without ever knowing even her real name.

Despite being knocked around by life and love, Abby has made a small life for herself as a hairstylist. She's content remaining on the sidelines of other people's special occasions, but it doesn't seem as if she'll ever be in line for a happily-ever-after of her own.

Dylan is on the Camdens' naughty list for bringing trouble into the close-knit family. Working to regain favor, he's pulled off a coup getting Abby and her special occasions team on board for his sister's quickie wedding. In the meantime, he also has to reveal to Abby who she really is.

But when Abby and Dylan hit it off, who Abby really is convinces her that she's that much less suited to getting involved with a Camden.

You'll have to read on to find out if the gap can be bridged. But I warn you, it's a bumpy ride.

I hope you enjoy it!

Always,

Victoria Pade

Abby, Get Your Groom!

Victoria Pade

◆ HARLEQUIN® SPECIAL EDITION®

Recycling programs
for this product may
not exist in your area.

ISBN-13: 978-0-373-65934-0

Abby, Get Your Groom!

Printed in U.S.A.

Victoria Pade is a *USA TODAY* bestselling author. A native of Colorado, she's lived there her entire life. She studied art before discovering her real passion was for writing, and even after more than eighty books, she still loves it. When she isn't writing she's baking and worrying about how to work off the calories. She has better luck with the baking than with the calories. Readers can contact her on her Facebook page.

Visit the Author Profile page at Harlequin.com for more titles.

Chapter One

"I can't get married looking like this!"

Dylan Camden heard his sister's lament as he went into the kitchen of his grandmother's home. He was coming from an apology lunch he hoped would gain him a few more good-grace points with his family. He had fences to mend and he was trying to act on every opportunity to do that.

But the minute he set eyes on his sister he couldn't help laughing before he caught himself and agreed with her. "You're right, that is *not* good hair."

It looked like a rats' nest with bows.

Lindie and Georgianna Camden—the grandmother they all called GiGi—turned at the sound of his voice.

"And this is the *third* try!" Lindie said. "Three different stylists from three different Camden Superstores salons. No wonder revenues in most of them are down if this is their quality of work!"

"I think I might have a solution that will kill two

birds with one stone," GiGi said. "You know about the visit from the prison chaplain—"

It had come as a surprise to everyone three days ago when a chaplain from the state penitentiary had shown up at GiGi's house in the heart of Denver's Cherry Creek. He'd come a long way with a request.

In the final week of longtime inmate Gus Glassman's life, Glassman had asked that the chaplain track down a lockbox of his belongings to be given to the daughter he'd abandoned twenty-eight years ago when he was incarcerated.

The incident that had caused the man to be imprisoned was something GiGi had read about in the recently discovered journals of her late father-in-law, the founder of the Camden fortune, H.J. Camden.

During their lives, H.J., his son Hank—who was GiGi's late husband—and GiGi and Hank's sons, Mitchum and Howard, had all been suspected of heavy-handed, unscrupulous business practices. Rumors and accusations had flown about ruthlessness, deceit, and callous, cold-blooded and unprincipled practices.

Nothing had ever been proven. And because GiGi and her ten grandchildren had never met with anything but loving care and kindness from the men, it hadn't been difficult to deny what had seemed like only false accusations.

Then H.J.'s journals were discovered, proving that all the accusations were true.

As a result, the current Camdens were trying to quietly seek out those who were wronged in the past—or their descendants—and atone in some way that wasn't disloyal to the men they'd all loved, and also didn't open the gates to unfounded lawsuits.

Gus Glassman had been sent to the Colorado State

Penitentiary for manslaughter when he—working as an enforcer for the Camdens—had gone too far while giving a beating to a factory supervisor who was trying to form a union. The beating was given on H.J.'s orders. GiGi had explored the possibility of making amends to the family of the man who had died, but he'd left no descendants so she'd moved on to other incidents.

But the prison chaplain had relayed information that there was another person caught in the fallout of Glassman's deadly errand. An innocent whose existence was unknown until Gus Glassman revealed it to the prison chaplain.

Gus Glassman had left behind a then-two-year-old daughter.

When GiGi heard that, she'd assured the chaplain that she would find the lockbox and Gus Glassman's daughter and take care of everything.

"I didn't want this to wait any longer so I've been looking into it since the minute I said goodbye to the chaplain," GiGi went on, "and you aren't going to believe it, Lindie—she's a stylist for that salon, Beauty By Design. The one that Vonni said a lot of her brides are using instead of Camdens."

"The one that advertises their special-occasion team?"

The seventy-five-year-old matriarch nodded. "The hairdresser who manages the shop and does the special occasion events is Abby Crane—"

"Gus Glassman's daughter," Dylan contributed. His cousin Cade had just told him over lunch—after Dylan's profuse apologies to Cade and Cade's wife, Nati. "But you can't be thinking that Lindie could find a way to make amends to her in the middle of this sprint to her wedding!"

"What I was thinking," GiGi said to him with that

putting-him-in-his-place tone that he recognized well, "is that if we could get this group to do the wedding, the girls might all get their hair done the way they want and in the process we'd be establishing contact with Abby Crane."

Mellowing her tone, GiGi included Lindie again as she went on. "According to the chaplain, Gus Glassman made sure his daughter wouldn't know who her father was, or anything about where she came from. All he left her with was a blanket and a note saying her name was Abby. But I have learned that she grew up in foster care, moved around from home to home—"

"No telling how happy or unhappy that might have left her," Dylan interjected. "She could be a pretty tough cookie. So let me do it. That's why I came by—Cade told me about what you'd found out. And I should be who does this project."

"You want your hair, makeup and nails done for the wedding?" Lindie goaded him.

"I could start with a haircut to get my foot in the door so I can tell her who she is," he suggested.

"But we also need someone to do wedding hair," GiGi reasoned. "That's two birds with one stone."

"And I'm in charge of security for the wedding—and security for everything leading up to it—and trying to keep the circus that's developed around this to a minimum," Dylan reminded her. The task was a natural fit for him, given his usual position as head of all Camden business security.

Lindie had met her fiancé, Sawyer Huffman, only a little over a month ago when GiGi had sent her on her own make-amends mission.

But Sawyer Huffman had made a career out of mounting very public opposition to every Camden Superstore being opened in the country. So when word had leaked that these two adversaries were coming together—coupled with the fact that any Camden major life event drew the media—it had caused a flurry of attention that was complicating the already problematical planning of a big wedding in a month's time. A month's time when they'd begun. Now the wedding was just over a week away.

"In order to have people outside of Camden Superstores doing anything with this wedding I need to find out if this woman can be discreet," Dylan reasoned. "I need to check out the salon to see if you girls can go in and get what you need done without photographers taking everyone's pictures through the windows—"

"And you *do* need a haircut before the wedding," GiGi commented.

"So give me this make-amends mission and I can start with a haircut. That'll get me in the door. Then I can approach Abby Crane about doing the wedding and to tell her that I know who she is. After twenty-eight years this shouldn't wait any longer. It has to be one of the worst things we've learned about what was done in the past," Dylan finished.

Both Lindie and GiGi sobered noticeably. It was clear to see they agreed.

"So let me take care of it," Dylan reiterated.

For a moment neither Lindie nor GiGi said anything.

Dylan wasn't sure whether that was due to the weight of what had happened twenty-eight years ago, or because no one in the family particularly trusted him these days.

Then, with some levity to her skepticism, Lindie said, "*You're* going to be the one to set up a hair-and-makeup trial for me and my bridesmaids?"

"Sure. Why not?"

"And you know that if we don't like what Abby does, we won't hire her, either, and that's going to make the other part a lot harder."

"I'm up for any challenge," he claimed.

"The first one will probably be scheduling your own haircut in a busy salon on short notice," Lindie said. "Let alone getting them to fit in a test run and an entire wedding party in just over a week."

"I'll do whatever it takes," he assured them.

Lindie looked to GiGi, who put Dylan under the kind of scrutiny she'd used on them when they were kids trying to bargain themselves out of punishment.

When Dylan didn't waver she seemed to give in without much enthusiasm and said, "Well, give it all a try and let's see how you do."

"And make it fast!" Lindie added, before she said she had to run and left Dylan alone with his grandmother.

Who returned to staring at him.

"Lunch went all right?" GiGi asked after they heard the front door close behind his sister.

"I think so. Nati wasn't really warm and fuzzy toward me, but she said she accepted my apology."

"And Cade?"

"We're okay. Nati had to be somewhere so she left right after lunch. Once she had, Cade said he was cutting me a little more slack than she was because we're family and he thought I'd had the wool pulled over my eyes. But that I should have known better…"

A sentiment that seemed prevalent among his entire family. "I agreed and by the time I paid the check things were more like always between us. He even said he'd work on softening up Nati a little more." Dylan paused, then said, "What about Jonah?"

Jonah was Nati's grandfather, and the high school

sweetheart GiGi had reconnected with and married several months ago.

"He told you that his granddaughter would never have been unkind to Lara," GiGi said with enough of an edge to her voice to make Dylan aware that she was still slightly miffed at him.

"I know, I know," he said. "But—I can only say it for the hundredth time—Lara was convincing, and I... blindly took her side..." Because he'd been in love with her.

"Jonah will be all right," GiGi admitted then. "He's forgiving—or how would he and I be together now?"

Because one of those long-ago Camden misdeeds had been done to him and his family.

"I can only say how sorry I am," Dylan repeated what he'd said more times than he could count.

"And we all see that you're trying to make things right again—that's important," GiGi said, the caring tone of a grandmother creeping into her voice to let him know that while she might not have appreciated what had happened to their family at the hands of his former fiancée, she still loved him. "It's just going to take time. We've never had that kind of thing go on among our own. We're used to battling what comes at us from the outside, but from the inside?"

"I know," Dylan repeated, willing now to accept the truth he'd denied. And to do whatever it took to get things back to where they were pre-Lara. To get himself back to where he was before he'd become the black sheep. And to make his own amends to his family.

GiGi patted his cheek gently, comfortingly. "You made a mistake, Dylan, but it'll all come out in the wash."

He nodded, hoping that was true. That he'd only rocked the boat.

That he hadn't knocked an irreparable hole in the side of it.

And that maybe doing one of these atonement-projects on behalf of them all would help.

Great hair. Great-looking guy... Abby Crane thought as she saw the man being led to her station on that Friday afternoon, the first week of October.

She was in the break room, wolfing down a late lunch between appointments. But she could see into the salon through the latticed partition that separated the two spaces.

After situating the superhunk, her best friend, China Watson—who was filling in for their receptionist today—joined Abby.

"That is *not* Betty Grove," Abby said.

Betty Grove, her scheduled appointment, was ninety and there certainly wouldn't be any mistaking her for the lean, muscular, broad-shouldered, six-foot-three man with the full head of lush, espresso-brown hair.

He wore it short on the sides, longer and in controlled disarray on top. And that was only the beginning of his appeal.

The guy had a squarish, angular, very masculine face with a sharp jawline and a just-prominent-enough chin. He had a slightly long but well-shaped nose, and lips that weren't too full or too thin lurking amid some very sexy stubble that told her he probably had to shave twice a day if he wanted to keep that altogether hella-handsome face perfectly smooth.

But unless he was going to do damage to some lucky girl's face when he kissed her, Abby thought, he shouldn't bother with a second shave because the stubble gave him an air of simmering sensuality and an irresistible bad-boy appeal.

"He's something, isn't he?" China said, as if she knew exactly what Abby was thinking. "He called for an appointment with you about forty-five minutes ago and he wanted in so bad he was offering to pay double if I'd work him in any way I could—"

"So you bumped Betty? Hasn't she had enough disappointments this week with her granddaughter calling off the wedding she paid for?"

"No, I didn't *bump* Betty. I put Mr. Beautiful on hold because I was going to come and see if you wanted to stay late. But just then Betty called to say she couldn't make it today—I guess Janette is a basket case from calling off the wedding and Betty doesn't want to leave her. Anyway, I got back on the phone with this guy, told him if he could make it here in twenty minutes he could have the appointment and there he is."

"He really did want in today. But I'm not seeing any reason for it to be an emergency," Abby observed, still studying him from the distance.

"His name is Dylan Camden—one of *those* Camdens, do you think?"

Abby shrugged. "I don't know. But if he is, why would Mr. Richie Rich be here? Or asking for me?"

"Word of mouth, Ab! You're good, and it's even getting around in elevated circles. So go show him your stuff!" China finished, her tone loaded with innuendo as she nudged Abby with her shoulder.

"You show him *your* stuff," Abby countered jokingly.

"He does *not* need makeup. But if I was the one he was so bent on seeing today, I'd show him plenty—look at him!"

Abby just shook her head at her friend.

"Are you going right out or should I keep him company?" China asked then.

"I'm going out. Just let me wash lunch off my hands."

"I'll ask him if he wants coffee or something…" China suggested, heading back the way she'd come as Abby got up from the table, threw away the paper plate she'd used and went into the employee's bathroom.

As she washed her hands she glanced in the mirror above the sink to make sure she looked okay.

But *not* because of the hot guy waiting for her.

Appearance was her line of work so she always wanted to look her best. It just seemed like a smart business practice.

Her own hair was dark, dark brown, too. And thick and curly. The long hair fell in spiraling curls that she parted slightly off-center and let fall to just below her shoulders. It made for a pretty full mass that she worked to keep from ever looking fried or frazzled or brittle.

Wearing it that long and full was something she hadn't been allowed to do growing up. When she was a little girl, the foster homes she'd been in had said it was too much trouble and shorn her like a sheep. But even when she'd gotten old enough to comb it herself the length and mass had still been an issue—one home had said it clogged the drain, another that it used up too much shampoo and conditioner. One set of foster parents had seen it as some kind of sign of wildness and degeneracy. But all of them had come to the same conclusion—keep it short.

She'd hated that. So now that she was an adult and on her own, she wore it exactly how she wanted it—long.

The good thing about it was that it was so thick it didn't go limp, even on Fridays like today, when she was booked solid. A few scrunches after her hands were dry and it had new life.

She just thought it accentuated her features better than when it was short. It provided a frame to her not-very-large face with its high cheekbones and fair skin.

To China's sorrow as a makeup consultant, Abby didn't wear much of it. Every day she applied only a little blush and a light dusting of brown eye shadow to go along with some mascara so that her almost-black eyes could compete with all the hair.

She thought her nose was a bit pointy, but at least it was straight, and she had just-full-enough lips that really only needed a little gloss.

She freshened that gloss now, before brushing cracker crumbs off of the black smock that protected her clothes and hid the body that was curvy but compact.

Then she popped a mint into her mouth and went back out to the salon, taking note that the oh-so-handsome guy in her chair wasn't looking at himself in the mirror he was facing. Instead, he was glancing around at the shop.

It told her something about the person and the level of vanity she was dealing with. Her impression of this guy was that he took those good looks in stride. She liked that.

"Hi, I'm Abby," she introduced herself when she reached her station.

"I know. Abby Crane—you're who I needed to see today," the hunk responded. "I'm Dylan Camden."

Abby went to stand in front of the chair to get a full forward view of him.

Wow, those eyes...she thought as she got close enough to see their color—vibrant, deep ultramarine blue. She'd never seen eyes a shade of blue that intense.

"Camden...like the stores? Or is that just a coincidence?" she asked, making conversation to break the ice.

"Not a coincidence," he answered.

So he *was* a Superstore Camden...

Why had a bigwig like that suddenly been so eager to get in to see her in her small, north Denver salon?

"How did you hear about us?" she asked out of curiosity.

"You. It's you I heard about," he amended. "First from my sister-in-law Vonni. She runs the wedding departments in our stores and she knows your work for special occasions. She's been finding that a lot of her brides and wedding parties are hiring you instead of using the salons in the Superstores."

"We like to go the extra mile for big events," Abby said, rather than bad-mouthing his salons.

"And you head that team."

"I do," she confirmed.

"Well, I'm here to talk to you about that, along with my own hair cut. My sister is getting married in about a week and she's in a bind when it comes to the whole hair thing—"

"And you're thinking *we* could do it? In 'about a week?'"

"I know it's ridiculously short notice and that you're in high demand, so what I'm asking is a big deal. But I'm willing to do all I can to make it work."

He *knew* that she was in high demand? There was something about the way he said it that made it sound like he thought he was some kind of authority on her.

But how could that be?

"Did you talk to China about all this when you called?" she fished.

"No, just about the haircut."

"But you *know* about my scheduling?"

"I know a few things about you. Things you can't know about yourself—"

"Such as?" Abby challenged him, suspicious.

"Such as, I know that when you were two years old you were left sleeping in the emergency department's waiting room of Denver General Hospital with nothing but a blanket and a note pinned to you that said your name was Abby."

How—*why*—would he know that? It wasn't as if she readily or easily opened up to anyone—clients, friends, dates, anyone. And she'd never met this man before. Plus he was a Camden. Why would someone from a family like that know those kinds of details about her?

"You get off on reading twenty-eight year old newspaper articles?" she asked.

"No, we…uh…had a different source. One closer than a newspaper article." His eyes met hers steadily. "But that's better talked about privately so I thought maybe we could set up a time to meet later, too—"

"Okay, what is this?" Abby demanded firmly, switching to the tough-girl tone she'd sometimes needed to use in rough foster homes.

He held up his hands, palms out. "Exactly what I've told you—I'm here for a haircut and to talk to you about my sister's wedding."

"And about something that you want me to meet you for later?"

"Because it's better talked about in *private*," he repeated, his voice quieter than hers had been.

China appeared from nowhere just then and Abby knew her friend had been lurking close enough to hear at least a portion of what had been said. China had probably only been hanging around to ogle the guy, but now any indication of admiration was gone. In its place was I've-got-your-back mode. China had also been a foster child and it was a pattern the two of them had developed when they'd become friends.

But even though Abby wasn't sure what was going on here, she didn't think it was anything she couldn't handle so she told China, "It's okay."

The tall, very blonde China looked from Abby to the man in her chair through narrowed hazel eyes that were always dramatically lined and shadowed.

To the client, China said, "If there's something fishy with you—"

"There isn't," he claimed, digging his wallet out of his back pocket. "Look, I am who I say I am." He handed Abby his driver's license and a business card. "And I'm honestly here with only the best intentions."

Abby looked over the license and card, then let China see them, too. When they were both finished with them he retrieved his license but left the card with Abby.

"Keep that. It has all my numbers on it—business and personal. I was going to leave it with you anyway so you could reach me after this."

Abby looked at China, who looked back at Abby, both of them confused but still suspicious.

Then China stepped out of Abby's station and seemed to disappear, though Abby had no doubt her friend would stay nearby.

"So, what's going on?" she demanded then.

"Right now, a haircut and talk about my sister's wedding," he said as if he were narrowing it down for the moment.

Abby was half tempted to refuse both and send him packing.

But she knew that if Sheila—the owner of two shops who left the managing of this one to Abby—heard that Abby'd had the opportunity to do the wedding of anyone as prominent as a Camden and refused, there would be hell to pay. It would likely cost her her job. So she had to at least hear him out.

"A haircut and talk about your sister's wedding," she reiterated.

"For now, here. And then maybe we can set up something for later so I can tell you the rest. Somewhere neutral, where you feel completely safe and can just listen to what I have to say."

Abby glared at him, again adopting her tough-girl attitude.

But once more she thought of how much she'd be risking if she didn't accept the business he was offering, so she signaled her shampoo boy to come and lead Dylan Camden to the sinks. She stayed where she was, watching from there and wondering what was up with this guy.

When he'd first confirmed his connection to the Camden Superstores, she'd wondered if he was there to offer her a job. She'd heard that the Camden salons were really slipping these days and it wouldn't be the first time someone had come in to steal her away from Sheila under the guise of having her do their hair.

But then he'd brought up the hospital. And he did seem to know things…

It was stupid. Totally stupid, and it hadn't happened in years and years and she hated herself for lapsing into some old childhood dream. But a stranger coming out of nowhere, knowing something about her past, saying he had more to tell her, provoked the old fantasy just the same.

The fantasy of someone appearing in her life unexpectedly to tell her she'd been misplaced by loving parents who had finally found her and wanted to whisk her away to somewhere she belonged. To a family she belonged to.

It was far-fetched. She knew it. And Dylan Camden was only a few years older than her own thirty so he certainly wasn't one of her long-lost parents.

But what if...

What if he was coming to tell her he was her brother? They both did have dark hair.

No, she decided. Dark hair was too common for her to draw conclusions just from that. And she certainly didn't have the signature blue eyes the Camdens were known for—the Camden Blue Eyes, the papers called them. They were even more striking in person than she'd expected.

But the Camdens were a big-deal family with a huge number of associates and connections. There were countless ways the Camdens could have known her parents. Could she be the daughter of a socialite friend who had had her when she was very young and ultimately given her away to avoid humiliation and embarrassment?

Pie in the sky, she told herself.

Pipe dreams.

Dumb.

But what if Dylan Camden really did know something—anything—about her background?

It wouldn't take much to know something she didn't. And just in case...

It was insanely far-fetched.

But even so, the longer she thought about it, the more she knew that she was going to agree to meet with him.

In order to find out if he really did have even a morsel of information about who she was.

Chapter Two

Dylan paid the bill for his haircut at Beauty By Design's reception desk then leaned around the partition behind it to call back to Abby Crane. "The park on Thirty-Second and Bryant, tonight at six-thirty, at the picnic tables—I'll find you," he said, repeating the time and location of the meeting she'd agreed to.

From her station she nodded that so-full head of shiny hair. He'd noted that it was the color of the Belgian bittersweet chocolate that he'd gorged on for the past three months.

"You'd better be on the up-and-up," muttered the receptionist.

"I am, don't worry," he assured her before leaving the salon.

It was only a little after four and Dylan knew he should go back to his office for a while. But as he got into his black Jaguar the thought of that just didn't sit well.

He wasn't far away—he was on the very outskirts of the city, and it wouldn't take him more than fifteen minutes to be sitting behind his desk again.

But since returning from three months of working on the security in the European stores—which he'd done to escape Lara and let the situation here cool off—everything seemed to require so much extra effort. It was taking its toll on him.

Sure, it was effort he was willing to put in. Effort he knew that he owed his entire family. And he definitely wanted to make things right again because he couldn't even put into words how much he hated the way things were between himself and the family now.

But it wasn't easy keeping up that eager-to-please attitude nonstop, day in and day out. It wasn't easy doing things like today's mea-culpa lunch with Cade and Nati—one of many he'd done during the three weeks since he'd been back. And sometimes he just needed to crawl to the back of his cave like a bear and take a few minutes before he could do more of it.

Like right now.

So rather than heading for the offices of Camden Incorporated where he would be around any number of siblings and cousins who were never particularly happy with him these days, he drove to his lower downtown penthouse loft instead.

There, he parked in his spot in the underground garage, rode the private elevator to the top floor and sighed in relief as he passed through the elevator's doors when they opened directly into his loft.

His cave wasn't very cave-like, admittedly.

The living room, dining room and kitchen were all one expansive open space decorated in glass, leather and chrome with mere hints of serene sky blue accents. The lines were smooth and there was no clutter. It was quiet, clean, and everything was in its place.

Lara had hated it.

And maybe that, and the fact that her own condo was decorated in what he'd considered "clutter chic," should have been an indicator that she thrived on chaos.

But like all the rest of the clues, he'd missed that one, too.

As nice as it was to be home, and as tempting as it was to just chill out until he needed to leave again to meet Abby, he realized that he still had to let his sister and grandmother know what was going on. It was part of being on his best behavior, after all.

He took his phone out of his pocket and walked to the wall of windows that allowed him a view of most of Denver. Lindie was first on the list, to tell her that he'd arranged for her and her bridesmaids to have the hair and makeup trial by the special occasions team of Beauty By Design.

Abby had said that she ordinarily took Wednesdays off, but after some persuasion—and a conference with China who was apparently the head of the makeup-artist portion of it all, and the manicurist in charge of the nail division—they'd all agreed to do the trial next Wednesday.

And, yes, due to a cancellation of a wedding on the same Saturday that Lindie's was scheduled, Abby Crane and the Beauty By Design group would be available for the race to the altar that Lindie had opted for, if Lindie and her bridesmaids were happy with the results of the test run.

Dylan concluded by relaying Abby's email address so his sister could send pictures and information about what she had in mind.

Then Dylan called his grandmother to tell her the same things, as well as that he was meeting with Abby tonight to open the door on her past.

Both Lindie and GiGi appreciated what he'd accomplished but there was still an edge of reserve, a chilliness, from both of them—the same thing he met from the rest of the family at the office every day. So he was glad when the calls were complete and he could do what he'd come home to do—relax and let down his guard.

But the way things were still weighed on him.

Everybody had been pretty ticked off by the time he'd ended things with Lara, when he'd left for Europe. And even now, after admitting he'd been wrong and apologizing until he was blue in the face, feelings were still hurt, tempers were still tweaked and things were still stilted.

He just had to keep chipping away at it and eventually maybe the whole thing would get to be history.

The way he and Lara were.

"Crazy-ass woman," he grumbled, reminding himself of his appointment on Monday to take the Jag into the shop to have the dents she'd made in it repaired.

If his siblings and cousins hadn't been so mad at him when he'd left for Europe one of them probably would have had it done while he was gone. But as it was, his car had been left sitting in the parking garage for three months, the way he'd left it, and now he had to get it taken care of.

Luckily he'd had the windshield replaced before he'd left so he could drive it now. But there was plenty of bodywork that needed to be done on the expensive sports car.

Just one more thing that was all messed up…

Now, in retrospect, he could see how it had gotten that way. Subtly. Insidiously. Quietly. He could see where he hadn't listened to what his family was saying and should have. He could see what he'd been blinded to by his feelings for Lara. He could see where he'd crossed the line himself on her behalf. And he sure as hell wished that he'd never given in to that urge in him to be her damn white knight.

But regrets and merely seeing things in retrospect weren't enough. There was a price to pay for what had happened.

He knew that. And he was willing to pay that price. But, unfortunately, payment was coming late. In the end, he'd had to escape to Europe for a while just to get out of Lara's sights himself—and that time lapse with his family had widened the gulf and made things all the more awkward to put back together again now.

He just had to keep at it, regardless of how rough it might be or how much he wished he could turn back the clock and stop it all from ever happening.

On the up side, he told himself, it had only taken Lara three months to get engaged to some other poor sucker. When he'd heard about the engagement he'd figured the coast was clear to come home, finally address things with his family and hopefully get them all back on track. It would have been worse if he'd been gone longer.

He hadn't seen or heard from Lara since he'd come home. Thank God! He had no desire to ever set eyes on her again as long as he lived.

And exhausting as it was to put back together everything she'd broken, at least he'd had a couple of wins today. Hopefully he'd gotten a few steps closer to being forgiven by arranging for one of the most highly reputed stylists around to work on his sister's wedding with very short notice—a coup if Lindie liked Abby Crane's work.

Plus he'd set the wheels into motion to relay to Abby

all his grandmother had told him so she could know where she'd come from. And he was on the path to find a way to compensate her somehow for what she'd suffered because of the actions of his family.

Assuming that Abby Crane had suffered.

But he did assume that, especially coming from his own current situation.

He'd felt lousy the past several months being on the outs with his family and a continent away from them. He'd been at loose ends the whole time. Adrift. He'd felt so damn cut off and alone in the world. It had been a rotten way to feel and he still didn't like the sense that he was being kept at arm's length, that he wasn't embraced by them all the way he was used to.

So what must it have been like for Abby Crane to grow up in foster care, moved from home to home, with no family of her own *ever*?

He couldn't imagine that it had been good for her.

And yet, she wasn't what he'd expected of someone who had been shuffled through the system.

He'd expected her to be hard-edged. He wouldn't have been surprised by spiked hair or tight leather or all-black clothes. By tattoos and piercings. By an I-dare-you-to-cross-me attitude.

But that wasn't Abby Crane.

Instead she was a fresh-faced beauty who looked as if she could have grown up in the country, on a farm.

A *spectacular* beauty, certainly without any obvious too-hard edges.

No, she was all soft curly hair—wild, thick hair that he'd kind of wanted to get his hands into. She was all smooth peaches-and-cream skin that didn't show signs of ever having had so much as a blemish.

She was all fine, delicate bones in a nose that not even

the most expensive plastic surgeon could have done as well. She had a slightly pointed, defined chin and high cheekbones dusted naturally pink and pretty.

And there definitely wasn't anything hard about her soft-looking lips or those big brown doe eyes that somehow sparkled even from that deep, dark color.

Why he hadn't expected someone quite that attractive to come out of the life she'd had he didn't know, but he hadn't. And he could honestly say that even if she had been on a rocky road in the past, it wasn't reflected in the way she looked now.

About the only possible indication of a difficult youth had been in the way she carried herself.

She was relatively small—not more than five feet four inches—and trim under that black smock. He'd seen that when she finished his haircut and took it off, revealing a body with tight curves in all the right places. But she stood straight and tall, shoulders back, head high, as if intent on making herself seem bigger than she was and strong enough to take on the world.

And there was nothing effusive about her—that probably came from the way she'd grown up. She was friendly enough but not overly so. Self-contained. And while she seemed warm toward that China person, he certainly hadn't felt an over-abundance of warmth directed at him.

She was slightly outspoken, too, he recalled, remembering her unabashed demand to know what he was up to. And she was no good at hiding the suspicion she'd felt. But that attempt to sound intimidating had just been adorable. Thinking about it made him smile the way he would have at the time if he hadn't suppressed it.

So if foster care had left scars they weren't readily visible. But it was something to watch out for anyway, he told himself. Like Lara's true nature hiding just under the surface, Abby could have plenty of baggage that wasn't easy to see but that could end up being hell to deal with.

Purely on a business level, of course. It wasn't as if he was considering anything else. Anything personal. There wasn't going to be anything personal between him and *any* woman for a long time. Not when he had so much damage control still to do with his family.

And even if he was ready for another relationship, even if all his fences with his family were mended, he'd be cautious of someone who came from Abby's kind of background. Stable, steady, grounded—that's what he'd be looking for when he started looking for someone again.

Someone who had been raised moving around from home to home? He didn't see how that could breed stable or steady or grounded.

Maybe that wild hair of Abby Crane's was the kind of clue that the clutter of Lara's condo should have been.

And this time around he was reading it, noting it, and taking it *very* seriously.

Not that there was anything to what he was about to do with Abby Crane that was at all relationship-driven to make that matter.

There wasn't.

His only job was to reveal to her who she was, where she'd come from, and then see how he could—in some way—make things up to her.

At the same time he was making things up to his family.

And, with any luck, maybe he could take care of everything at once and then *really* breathe a sigh of relief.

But no matter how long either chore took, it was all

going to be far behind him before he even considered getting involved with another woman.

Fresh-faced spectacular beauty or not.

The park on Bryant Street was only a block from Abby's apartment. She wanted to walk there but it was after six o'clock when she got home so she had to hurry in order to change clothes first.

Not that she really needed to change clothes—there was nothing wrong with what she'd been wearing all day. And she convinced herself that it wasn't for the sake of Dylan Camden. She just felt like putting on something fresh.

So she replaced her work jeans with a better pair that were low-slung and fitted her rear end just the way she liked. On top she opted for a slimmer-cut black T-shirt that hugged her not overly well-endowed chest. She wore that over a white-and-black polka dot tank top that rose about two inches higher than the T-shirt's square-cut neckline.

She drew a large hair pick through her curls and re-scrunched them, and refreshed her eye makeup, blush and lip gloss. Although she probably shouldn't have used the time, she searched out and put on a pair of hoop earrings before rushing back to her closet for shoes.

Despite telling herself that she should wear sturdy shoes in case this guy was some kind of creep she might need to kick before making a run for it, she still went with a pair of ballet flats that wouldn't be able to do any damage.

But they were comfortable and she'd been on her feet all day. Plus they had cute little white-and-black polka dot bows that coordinated with her tank top.

It was six-twenty-five by then, so she grabbed her

keys, put them in the pocket of her jeans and headed for the park.

Dylan was already there—Abby spotted him when she reached the corner across the street from the park. He was sitting at one of the picnic tables. And looking as good as he had at the shop that afternoon.

She'd been hoping that maybe he wouldn't. That the flattering lighting of the salon had just really worked for him. But that wasn't the case. The guy was sooo hot!

But that wasn't going to get to her. He was still a stranger and her guard was up on that account alone. But there were two other things that factored in, too— she'd just ended the only long-term relationship she'd ever been in, and what had come out of it had shaken her. *That* wasn't anything she wanted to try again any-time soon.

And if she hadn't been good enough for Mark The Systems Analyst, she certainly wouldn't be able to live up to the standards of a Camden. Someone like that would surely believe he was legions out of her league.

So, Adonis or not, Dylan Camden wasn't going to get to her.

He saw her coming just then and perked up as if he was happier to see her than she thought he should be. Or maybe he'd just thought she wouldn't show and was glad she had. But she was still leery.

"Hi," she said as she drew near the table.

"Hey there," he responded.

He was sitting on the table itself, his big loafered feet on the bench below, long jeans-encased legs V'd out wide, leaning on forearms atop thick thighs—nicely developed forearms exposed below the rolled-up-to-his-elbows sleeves of a crisp, clean, pinstriped shirt.

He'd changed clothes, too. And he'd shaved so his

face was clear of stubble, as if he wanted to be ready for kissing.

Dumb thought. Surely he hadn't shaved so he'd be ready for kissing *her*.

"Shall we walk or sit here?" he asked when she joined him.

"Let's just sit," she said, preferring to stay near to the busy street and her apartment.

"Oh, right, you work on your feet all day—taking a walk is probably not high on the list of things you want to do," he reasoned.

Sure, let him think that.

He stood then, and Abby was struck once more by how tall he was and what a great body he had—lean and toned, muscular, and wow, those shoulders and the way they tapered down to that narrow waist were impressive!

He motioned for her to sit on the now-free bench but she rounded the table and sat on the other side instead.

Something about that distance she put between them made him smile as he slung a long leg over the seat he'd just offered her and took it himself. And when he smiled small lines fanned out from the corners of his astonishingly blue eyes and drew the most appealing little parentheses around that supple mouth.

She tried not to notice, let alone appreciate the sight, but it was almost impossible *not* to appreciate someone who looked as good as he did.

"How's the hair?" she asked, letting herself look at him even more closely for a moment to assess the work she'd done on him earlier.

"Best haircut I've ever had," he said without equivocation. "I washed it in the shower, ran a towel over it when I got out and barely had to touch it from there."

She fought the mental picture of him in the shower—

and out of it. Naked. Big and strong and tight. Hard muscles glistening wet. Reaching those impressive arms up to rake a towel over that dark, thick hair and making those massive shoulders stretch while the sinews of his back flexed all the way down to those great glutes she'd caught a peek of when he'd left her station today…

Whew! That was not something she should be thinking about, either! And she wasn't quite sure where all those details had come from.

She chased the image out of her mind, forced herself to sound cool, detached and objective—which was not how she was feeling—and said, "It isn't too short… your hair?" she added, reminding herself that that was all she was supposed to be considering.

"Yeah, shorter than I wanted it but you were right to do it. It looks better than it ever has."

She didn't know about *ever* but she did know he looked fantastic there in the late-day, early-autumn sunshine. She restrained herself to say nothing more than an aloof, "Good, I'm glad you like it."

"My sister is thrilled that you can fit her and her bridesmaids in for the test run Wednesday," he said then. "And that if that goes well, that you're free to do the wedding the Saturday after that. Her hopes are high and I told her I didn't think you'd disappoint."

"We'll do our best," Abby assured, effectively ending the catching-up part of things.

Which, she thought, left them with the reason he'd wanted this meeting. So she waited for him to get to it.

He must have realized it was time for that because he reached into one of his front pockets and produced a key that he held out to her.

She didn't take it. Instead she narrowed her eyes at

him and said, "If that's the key to your place and this is all some kind of come-on—"

"It isn't," he said quickly, setting the key on the picnic table closer to her than to him.

But rather than explaining what the key was for, he said, "Is there anything you know about where you came from? Your family or history or anything?"

"I know the same things you said this afternoon—I was left sleeping on a chair in the hospital waiting room with a blanket and a note saying my name was Abby. Someone along the line added Crane as my last name because there were pictures of cranes on the blanket that I guess I wouldn't let go of."

"I'd wondered where that came from."

"I know that local newspapers did articles and news stations did broadcast stories asking anyone who might be able to identify me to come forward," she went on, "and no one did. I know that there wasn't any information other than my first name so I've never had a real birth date. The pediatrician who checked me out at the hospital decided I was *barely* two so they picked a day the month before I was found and that's what I use when I have to give my date of birth. And that's it. That's all I know."

"I hadn't even thought about a birth date," Dylan muttered more to himself than to her.

"Apparently neither did whoever left me."

"And you don't remember anything?" he asked.

"I was, as far as anyone could tell, barely two years old. Do you remember anything from when you were two?" Abby countered.

He shook his head. "No, I don't think so."

"When I think about it, sometimes I get a vague sort-of sense of being somewhere with too many bright lights and being scared. But it's really just like a kind of faint dream. I've always figured that might be from waking up in the hospital with no one around that I recognized, but I'm not even sure if it's really a memory or if it's just how I imagine it was."

Dylan's handsome face had sobered considerably as she'd talked and his well-shaped eyebrows were drawn together in a troubled expression before he said, "It was your father who left you at the hospital."

"And you know this how? Because he was connected in some way to your father?"

"Yes, my family did play a part in you being abandoned…"

He sounded loath to admit that.

Then he said, "Your father is—was—a man named Gus Glassman. Ring any bells?"

"None," she answered honestly. Why had he corrected himself to say her father *was* Gus Glassman instead of *is*? Had he changed his name, or was he…no, she shouldn't get ahead of herself. She needed to pay attention to what Dylan was saying.

"Well, that key came from him." Dylan nodded at it. "Gus gave it to a prison chaplain just before he died—"

"Gus Glassman—my father—is dead?"

"I'm afraid so. I'm sorry," Dylan said with more sympathy, pausing a moment as if out of respect. Or maybe to let it sink in—which was what Abby was trying to let it do.

But it wasn't easy. These were just words to her. There were no instant emotions the way she'd thought there would be.

"According to the chaplain," Dylan went on, "he was the first person Gus ever told about abandoning you. He asked the chaplain to find you, to find the lockbox that this key opens and to give the contents to you."

"So where's the chaplain?" Abby asked.

"He came looking for Camdens because there's a connection. And talking to the Camdens means going to GiGi, first and foremost... GiGi is what we call my grandmother. She's the head of the family."

"A prison chaplain just showed up on the doorstep of the *foremost* Camden with this story and a key to a lockbox? Why? What does your family have to do with it?"

"We actually just found that out ourselves. Recently, we learned that twenty-eight years back your father worked for Camden Superstores. He was on the payroll as store security, but he did more than that..." Dylan said quietly, as if it was something else he didn't want to admit.

"What more did he do?" Abby asked, feeling removed from what he was telling her, still just trying to absorb it.

"It looks as if, when there was something brewing somewhere that could turn into a headache for some part of the business, my great-grandfather—H.J. Camden— had a few chosen men he sent in to...well, to do whatever it took to contain things before they got out of hand."

Dylan didn't seem proud of that because he was again talking quietly. "I guess you could say they were his... enforcers." That word came out more under his breath than out loud. "We have a lot of production factories. A supervisor in one of those factories was trying to unionize."

"And you didn't want it," Abby guessed.

"I was five, going on six—what I wanted was probably cookies and candy and to play outside. But no, H.J.—along with my grandfather and my dad and my uncle, who all ran the Superstores together—didn't want unions in the factories." Dylan's eyebrows arched toward his hairline in reluctance to say what he was going to say. "They wanted the labor leaders discouraged—"

"And Gus Glassman—my father—was the discourager?"

"Yeah. But that *discouragement* got pretty heated. It turned into an all-out fight between Gus and the supervisor, and in the course of that fight the supervisor fell back, hit his head and died."

"So my father was a thug? He was your family's bully or henchman or something, and he *killed* someone?" The fantasy of learning about her family had never included *that* and Abby was beginning to feel slightly knocked for a loop by the reality.

"I don't know that your father was a *thug* or a *bully* or a *henchman*," he said as if those terms were too harsh. "But he was involved in a bad situation, following orders that he probably shouldn't have been given. We— my grandmother, my siblings, my cousins and I—read about it in my great-grandfather's journal. We checked to see if the supervisor had left family or someone we should compensate—he hadn't. But when it came to Gus Glassman—"

"He was nothing but the guy who did your family's dirty work?"

It wasn't as if Abby felt any kind of affection for the man Dylan Camden kept calling her father, but she had too much experience being in positions where *she'd* been looked at as a nothing herself and he'd touched a nerve.

"No. What I was going to say was that when it came to Gus, we could contact him directly. So that was what we did—GiGi wrote to him, asking if there was anything we could do for him and if he'd left anyone behind who he might like us to reach out to."

"And he didn't say me," Abby said quietly.

"He didn't answer the letter at all. So GiGi found his attorney, who said that Gus had been a widower with no kids so we shouldn't worry about it. I guess not even the attorney knew about you."

Because she'd been a nothing even to her own father?

That thought didn't boost her spirits.

More and more feelings were coming at her but they were all jumbled and indecipherable as Dylan continued. "Like I said, telling the chaplain was the first time he'd so much as spoken of you since the supervisor's death. He told the chaplain that that was because he wanted to *spare* you having to grow up with the disgrace of a dad who had taken another person's life, who was convicted of manslaughter and sent to prison. He didn't want that following you around. The chaplain said your father was ashamed of what he'd done, that he'd never forgiven himself and that he didn't want to pass that shame on to you. He thought that you'd be better off just left somewhere—somewhere safe, because he knew you'd be taken care of in a hospital—without a last name or any information that could link you back to him."

So he *had* cared about her? He *had* thought about her welfare in whatever skewed fashion?

More feelings came, bringing with them more confusion.

It must have shown on her face because out of nowhere Dylan said, "I know it's kind of hard to reconcile things that don't seem to go together. I loved my great-grandfather, my grandfather, my dad and my uncle. They were unfailingly good to me. But I can't say I'm proud of all the things they did outside of the family. It's something we're all having to come to grips with. For us, we never forget that those same men who didn't always behave honorably were still people we loved, who loved us, so we have to separate things. And it seems like—in spite of what your dad went to jail for doing—he really did care about you. Maybe that's something to hang on to."

"Maybe…" she parroted, struggling with it all. Struggling, too, with the fact that this was so completely different than any of the romanticized thoughts she'd always entertained about where and who she'd come from, about why she'd been left.

But here she was, with Dylan Camden at the moment and she wasn't sure where this was supposed to go.

So she asked. "I guess, then, you'll tell me where to find the lockbox and that's it?"

"Well, if you'll let me, I'd like to help you piece together what we can of your background," Dylan said. "Figure out more about where you came from and the kind of man Gus Glassman was—because I have hope that he might have been a loving dad to you, despite what he did. Maybe we can figure out who your mom was, what happened to her and any family she might have had. It just seems like you should know as much as you can from here."

Should she? Abby wondered.

She wasn't sure.

In some ways she wanted to deny that this could actually be her background and step away from it as if it wasn't really hers.

It had been difficult enough growing up a foster kid. She'd been vigilant about being a good girl in order to live down preconceived notions about what that might mean.

And now to learn that she really was what some people had assumed—if not bad herself, then at least the child of a criminal? The daughter of someone who had *killed* someone else? Someone who had died in *prison*?

A part of her did not want to embrace it.

But it didn't seem as though that was possible.

"How would we do those things you said?" she asked, buying herself more time to think while her head was swimming.

Dylan nodded toward the key on the table again. "Gus told the chaplain that the lockbox that that key opens is hidden in *the store*—meaning one of our Superstores. We're trying to figure out which one he might have worked out of and locate the box. Hopefully that will give us more to go on. Plus, I run the security department for the Camden Superstores, and part of my job is to do background checks on people we hire. I have full access to our employee files, even the ones from before my time. If Gus was married to your mother I can find record of it and get your mother's maiden name—that would give us a starting point to looking into that side of your family."

"What about the chaplain? Where did he go in all of this?" Abby asked.

"He's from the prison in Canon City so he went back there. When GiGi heard what he had to say, she swore to him that we would take care of this."

"By hiring me to fix your sister's hair for her wedding?" Abby asked because she was trying to fit the pieces together.

"No. This and the wedding are not connected. Your reputation for your work preceded you. Or, at least, the work of the special occasions team from Beauty By Design preceded you. Then it just happened that the same name GiGi finally put to Gus Glassman's daughter was one of the names included on that team."

"So it's only a coincidence?"

"It honestly is. My haircut today was my chance to meet you, but even if you had turned down the wedding, you and I would still be here right now and I'd still be asking you to let me help you find out about your family. The fact that you agreed to do what you're doing for Lindie—on such short notice—is a whole separate thing." Under his breath, he muttered, "One that I'm hoping will get me some much-needed brownie points."

She didn't know what that meant so she didn't comment.

Then he said, "So, what do you think? I'm sorry I haven't brought you a happier story, but will you let me help you, anyway?"

Abby merely sat there looking at him, trying hard to absorb all he'd told her, trying to deal with it, considering what he was asking.

Did she want to know more if it was as sordid as what she'd just learned? Because this was *not* the fairy tale she'd always envisioned. And what if what went with it was worse?

But there was that key on the table between them and the knowledge she already had. And after a lifetime of not knowing anything, she knew she couldn't just ignore the chance to find out whatever more she could, good or bad.

"I'll be right by your side every step of the way," Dylan said then, as if he was reading her mind.

And Abby found that assurance that she wouldn't be alone in the process of uncovering her history somehow comforting.

Which was all the more confusing because she prided herself on standing on her own two feet to face whatever she had to face. The most support she'd ever had had been from China and this wasn't China. This was a stranger she'd just met today.

But here was this guy offering to help her and stick by her, and it made the whole delving-into-her-history thing more palatable.

It had been a really strange day...

"Okay, I guess," she heard herself say without any conviction whatsoever.

"Great!" he decreed. "I already have people looking for the lockbox, so that—and my digging through old marriage records—is where we'll start."

Abby nodded, feeling slightly shell-shocked.

"And in the meantime, Lindie's wedding is pulling a lot of attention from newshounds and I also have to keep a handle on that. Is there any chance that you and I can take an after-hours look through your salon so I can get a feel for how I can make sure the test run can be kept private?"

He'd moved on. It took Abby a moment to realize that and switch gears, too.

But she did.

"We don't do the special occasions work at the salon," she informed him. "The owner—Sheila—has two salons and there's a third location midway between the two where we *only* do the special occasions work. It makes it so our brides and their wedding parties—or whoever else we're working with for a special event—can spread out and get a little pampered without regular clients around."

"Then can you give me a tour of that place so I can check it out? The sooner the better."

He was really expecting a lot of her in her befuddled state. But she tried to think about work and scheduling and finally came up with an answer. "I guess I could meet you there tomorrow night—I know it's Saturday night but I'm booked from early tomorrow morning until closing at the shop so that would be the soonest… I know it's probably a date night for you with your girlfriend or wife or whatever, but—"

"There's no girlfriend or wife or date night or whatever. Would meeting with me be messing with any of that for you?"

"Me?" she said as if that was unthinkable. "No. There's none of that for me right now, either."

"Then we can do it tomorrow night?"

"I'll text you the address and directions. I can probably be there by seven."

"Seven it is, then," he agreed. "Now, how about that burger place over there? Can I buy you dinner?" He pointed his sculpted chin in the direction of a small redbrick building that housed two restaurants just in front of the old Victorian house where Abby rented a studio apartment.

Clearly he had no idea how overwhelmed she was if he thought there was any way she could be good company right now. She declined the invitation with the polite excuse that she'd promised to eat with China tonight.

"I'll see you tomorrow night, then," Dylan said without seeming to take any offense from the rejection.

They both stood and as he did, he picked up the key from the picnic table. "I think you should hang on to this."

This time Abby took it from him, her fingers brushing his as she did and making her oddly aware of some kind of heat passing between them.

"Are you okay?" he asked then, as if he'd just noticed that she was a little dazed.

"I'm fine. There's just been a lot that came at me all of a sudden…"

"Why don't you at least let me drive you home."

Abby took a deep breath of the evening air to clear her mind and shook her head. "I'm only a block away. The walk will do me good."

"Are you sure?" he asked skeptically.

"I am," she said, wondering if she should thank him or something.

But she didn't feel altogether grateful for what she'd learned tonight, so instead she just said goodbye and headed back the way she'd come.

It was only as she walked home that she recalled feeling somehow strengthened by the thought of picking through her past with him by her side.

Why would that have happened? she asked herself when it struck her as weird all over again.

It certainly couldn't have anything to do with the fact that he was fabulous looking—even though she suddenly found herself happy to think that she'd be seeing him again tomorrow night.

Maybe it was just because he was a big, strong guy who gave the impression that he could handle himself and anything thrown at him.

Except that whatever got thrown would be thrown at *her*…and so far, he'd been the one doing all the throwing.

But still, that must be it, she decided.

Because after all, what else *could* it be?

Certainly not that she was *attracted* to him.

They were worlds apart and she knew better than to try crossing over from her world to anyone else's.

Chapter Three

"So... Dylan Camden didn't come to tell you you're the secret, illegitimate daughter of a high-society socialite."

Like Abby, China fantasized a lot of scenarios for her friend that had extravagant happy endings.

It was early Saturday morning. After years of sharing an apartment to make ends meet when they'd aged out of foster care, Abby and China now had their own studio apartments across the hall from each other in a north Denver Victorian house that had been converted into an apartment building.

China had been on a date on Friday night and had come home too late for Abby to tell her about the meeting with Dylan. But the minute China woke up this morning she'd padded across the hall in her pajamas and bare feet to hear what Abby had learned.

Abby had told her the whole thing over coffee and cereal at her small pedestaled kitchen table.

"What do you think is in the lockbox?" China asked then. "A million dollars in gold coins? Another key and the number of a safety deposit box full of diamonds? A will that makes you—"

"Queen of a small country?" Abby finished with a laugh. "Somehow I don't think being the abandoned daughter of someone who rich people used to strong-arm their employees leads to stuff like that." And she didn't want to entertain any more hopes for anything. Not after suffering the kind of crash she'd had last night when it finally sank in that the real story of her past was so much seedier than she'd ever imagined.

She turned her open laptop so China could see the screen. "I looked up old newspaper articles on Gus Glassman last night. Here's his picture."

"Oh, well, no wonder you're gorgeous—you came from good genes," China said the minute she saw the photograph. "But you didn't get your dark eyes or dark curly hair from him—his eyes are lighter and the hair is straight and sandy brown. You have his nose and mouth, though. Anything about him look familiar?"

Abby shook her head. "Other than that little bit of resemblance, no. There were no flashes of looking up at him from my crib."

"He has nice eyes. I wouldn't be afraid to date him if I met him somewhere. He doesn't look like someone who could *kill* someone else," China said.

Abby knew her friend was searching for the positive side. But the facts didn't seem to bear that out.

"The articles back up what Dylan told me," she said. "Except that Dylan made it sound more like an accident and the articles don't. Gus had threatened the supervisor before—often enough that the supervisor had gone to the police about him because he was worried about his safety."

"If the cops didn't do anything they must not have thought your father was too scary."

"The police told the supervisor there was nothing they could do but file a report. But there was one article that said the police were on the side of the Camdens so they *wouldn't* do anything *because* the Camdens were involved—like the police were in their pocket or something."

"They *are* rich and powerful…" China said over her coffee cup.

"The supervisor's factory was taking a vote that day about whether or not to unionize. If that factory had voted to do it, it seemed like the workers in the other factories would, too. Gus—"

"He's your father, you know? You could call him that."

"It just doesn't seem like it," Abby admitted. Despite all the years she'd thought about someone coming to claim her, now she wasn't sure she wanted to claim him.

But she didn't tell China that. When China was seven years old she'd found her mother dead from a drug overdose on the kitchen floor. With no idea who her father was and no other family, China had gone into the system. But she remembered her mother and the time they'd had together. She loved her mother in spite of the addiction that had killed her and put China in situations that China still had nightmares about. Through it all, China still claimed her.

Given that, it made Abby feel a little ashamed to admit that she wasn't eager to do the same with Gus Glassman, that she didn't feel much other than shame for what she'd come from.

Rather than calling him her father or Gus Glassman, she said, "He was at the factory to intimidate the supervisor so the vote wouldn't be held. Employees testified that they were all afraid when they saw him. When he walked in, a lot of them decided not to vote at all. But the supervisor stood up to him and..." Abby shrugged. "They fought. The supervisor was killed. The newspaper articles also said that Gus had a police record stretching back to when he was a teenager. It was for minor things but still—"

"Okay, so he wasn't a saint. But if he was a good dad to you for those two years, that's something."

Abby knew that was how her friend would look at it because that was how China viewed her own years with her mother, forgiving her mother everything because her mother had loved her. But China's mother had done most of her harm to herself. She hadn't killed someone else.

"At least I guess I can be glad that Mark isn't around for this," Abby said then.

"I'm glad he isn't, too. He'd just make you feel worse about it!"

That was true enough.

"It's kind of hard to feel good about it, though," Abby confessed then. "Look farther down in the article—there's a picture of the supervisor."

China did.

"He looks like he was a nice guy, doesn't he? The article said he was a devoted member of his church. That he worked with the church's youth group and was a volunteer with Big Brothers—that means he was someone who tried to help kids like us. He was about the age we are now when he died. He had his whole life ahead of him and my father took it from him."

"Okay, your father did something bad. But maybe

he wasn't a bad person. You know I trashed that mean girl's bike when I was ten, but that didn't make me bad through and through, did it?"

"The mean girl was *sooo* mean to you," Abby commiserated, having heard the story about the year of constant abuse her friend had taken at the hands of the other kid. "But this isn't the same," she insisted. "And I don't know, China. I know I should just be happy to find out *something* about myself. But—"

"You hoped it would be something to be proud of. But what were the odds, Ab? How many kids in foster care over the years did you run into with the kind of stories we've made up about you?"

"None," Abby admitted.

"It's like everything else about us—we have to take what we can get and make the best of it."

"Because if we reach for more, like I did with Mark, we live to regret it," Abby added.

"That guy was a jerk who didn't appreciate what he had. Maybe the Camden hottie is smarter than that."

Abby was grateful for her friend's loyalty but it didn't change the facts. "Right," she said facetiously. "Like there would ever be anything between the *Camden hottie* and me. You and I also know what it means to be in the system and the way people see us because of that— even *before* they hear something like this."

Add to that the status and prestige of a *Camden*? She hadn't even been good enough for an upper-middle-class systems analyst like Mark. She'd really be barking up the wrong tree with Dylan! And it was something she knew she had to keep in mind now.

Now, when—despite having so much to think about with her suddenly disclosed past—she'd still found herself also thinking about Dylan Camden. And recalling every detail about that face and body. And mentally replaying everything he'd said and the sound of his voice as he'd said it. And picturing his every expression, his every gesture, his every nuance. She even kept closing her eyes and remembering how his cologne smelled like a forest filtered through clean mountain air, and the way his hair had felt when she'd cut it, for crying out loud!

"If you don't want to give him a chance does that mean I can?" China challenged her, yanking Abby out of the reverie she'd drifted into.

"No," Abby said quickly and firmly, making her friend laugh.

"I didn't think so," China said, as if she'd known it all along. "And our hottie wants to help you find out everything you can about your family?"

Abby tried not to recoil at the *our* part of that and say he was *her* hottie. Which he wasn't. But for some reason she was inclined to make that possessive correction and had to fight not to.

"I think Dylan and his family are on some kind of guilt trip over this," she said instead.

"Well, that says something good about them, doesn't it? They—or at least their relatives—were the ones who put the wheels into motion that left you without anyone to take care of you. Somebody *should* feel guilty about that."

"To answer your question—yeah, Dylan wants to help find out whatever can be uncovered." And to be by her side when they learned about her family—Abby kept coming back to that and to how much she liked it.

Well, how much she *appreciated* it. It wasn't that she could let herself *like* that he'd be with her.

Because she was out of her depth with him, she repeated to herself like a mantra.

And it was bad enough that she kept having that sense of him as some kind of reinforcement, she certainly couldn't let herself come to depend on it in some way. She knew better than to depend on anyone. Well, anyone except China.

"I'm still gonna keep my fingers crossed that he digs up good stuff," her friend said. "Maybe not gold coins or diamonds or a crown, but all good stuff from here, and that you've learned the worst there is to learn."

"I'm gonna hope for that, too," Abby said.

"But since today isn't the day somebody waved a magic wand and made us rich, I guess we'd better get dressed and go to work, huh?" China said then, glancing at Abby's wall clock.

They both stood and took their coffee cups and cereal bowls to the sink.

"Want to get a pizza tonight?" China asked in the process.

"I promised to meet Dylan at the special events shop after work to show it to him—he needs to check it out for security because he says this wedding has stirred up media interest or something. I don't know how long that will take."

"I'd say I'll wait for you but maybe he'll take you somewhere after…"

"It's just business. The family wedding and this looking-into-my-background thing—that's all there is to it and all there's going to be to it," Abby insisted.

China smiled. "Still, I don't want you committed to pizza with me, just in case."

Abby rolled her eyes as she put their cups and bowls in the dishwasher and her friend left.

But she was aware that she hadn't jumped in to insist that China wait for her tonight, to tell her friend she would make sure she was home in time for them to have dinner together.

Because even though it would actually give her an excuse she could use with Dylan to hurry him through the tour, deep down she didn't really want to shorten her time with him by even a minute.

"Okay, you're right—I can't see through those curtains even with the lights on in here," Dylan said after stepping out the front door of Beauty By Design's special occasions location and then rejoining Abby inside.

"And we only open the curtains if the wedding or party or whatever is going to be held outside. If it is, we need to make sure the makeup works in sunlight. But if we need the makeup to work in interior lighting, we need sunlight *not* to be a factor. Since your sister's wedding won't be outside—"

"You'll keep the curtains closed and photographers won't be able to take snapshots from the sidewalk if word happens to get out that this is where we are."

"Right."

"And there's parking and a door we can use in back rather than coming in through the front. Once the whole group is here I can lock both the front and the back doors because there won't be any other clients coming in and out," he repeated what she'd told him as she'd given him the tour. "I think that's everything, and this should be okay," he said then, taking one more glance around the opulent-looking open space designed to accommodate private groups having their hair, nails and makeup done.

Unlike either of the other two Beauty By Design shops that could accommodate fifty customers at a time, here there were only two pedicure chairs and manicure tables, and three stations where hair and makeup were done.

Also unlike the regular salons, there was a raised platform surrounded on three sides by full-length mirrors in case anyone wanted to try on their dress or gown for the full effect.

Plus there was a section in one corner with a huge, comfy white sofa and two matching chairs situated around a coffee table where patrons could relax between services and enjoy the finest chocolates along with cocktails, wine or champagne—or other beverages if the group was underage for a birthday, prom, sweet sixteen, bat mitzvah or quinceañera.

The object was to pamper clients in a party-like atmosphere that would be as much fun as the event itself while still making them look and feel beautiful.

"But I'm supposed to ask," he said, "if you end up doing the wedding—can it be done by you and your team coming to us rather than the wedding party coming here?"

"It costs extra."

He grinned, and she tried not to like the look of it as much as she did. But that attempt failed because a smile just added so many new elements to how good-looking he was and she couldn't help noting that.

"The cost doesn't matter if you'll just do it," he assured.

"We do that, yes," Abby responded. "In fact, I like when we get to."

"Really?" he asked as he leisurely climbed the steps up to one of the pedicure chairs—and in the process gave her a glimpse of some pretty spectacular male buns in a pair of jeans that knew just how to show off his rear end. Abby caught herself looking where she shouldn't have been just as he turned to sit and she shot her gaze upward.

Since he seemed to be settling in and she was in no rush, she went to sit in the other pedicure chair, angling toward him as he did the same so they were facing each other.

"Really," she confirmed. "If we do everything here, that's the end of it for me. The client goes off to have their special day, but I don't get to see any of it. If we do the work at the event we get to see more and be more involved in occasions that I'd never get to be a part of otherwise."

"You don't think you'll ever get married?" he asked, sounding surprised.

"Even if I do it can't possibly be on the scale that your sister's wedding will be. And the other stuff—proms and the coming-of-age celebrations, the Debutante Ball—those are things I never got to have, no."

"You never went to a prom?"

She shook her head then motioned with it to their surroundings. "I also never knew anyone who could pay for something like this. But now I get to participate in these big, fancy things indirectly. If we go to the venue I usually have the chance to peek in to see the flowers or the decorations or the cake. If we're hired to stick around for hair changes and makeup retouches, I get to hear the music, sometimes some of the food gets sent to us—we aren't guests but we get to experience some of it on the sidelines, and…" she shrugged "…that's fun for me. These are some of the happiest, most joyful and hopeful times in people's lives and I get to be a part of it. I get to help make it special, to make them look and feel beautiful for it, sometimes I get to see it—how nice is that?"

"I think it's nice that that's how you look at it," he

said, studying her as if he was getting insight into her. "Is that why you became a stylist?"

Abby laughed. "You're so funny to think there were a lot of choices in what I could become."

"You're smart, talented—"

"And you think that made a lot of difference?" she asked, even as she took his words as a compliment and reveled in the possibility that that might be what he thought of her. "When I was thirteen," she went on, "I needed to pick whether I planned to get a job right out of high school or if I wanted to try to go to college or trade school."

"At *thirteen*?"

"It isn't easy for kids in the system to follow the same course as kids with families who can afford to just let things play out. The world is not our oyster. So school counselors and case workers and just about every adult I ever came into contact with, warned me that I needed to plan for myself—"

"Starting at *thirteen*?"

"That was how old I was when I went to middle school. Before that, everybody learns the same things. But when I had to start picking some of my own classes, I needed to start thinking realistically about whether I wanted to go to college or trade school or just get a job. For me, trade school seemed like the middle of the road—something I was reasonably sure I could get into and afford with subsidized tuition, and something that wouldn't take as long as college before I could come out with some kind of skill to support myself."

"So you didn't choose to be a stylist at thirteen, you just chose trade school."

"Right. Which meant I wasn't put in the same classes as kids aiming for college."

"What if you had changed your mind?"

"I could have. But when I sort of toyed with the idea of college a few years later it was discouraged. My grades were good enough to get in somewhere, but my counselor said if I did, how was I going to pay for it? And how was I going to make enough money to live, too? Scholarships, grants, living stipends—things like that aren't a guarantee. I was warned not to plan on them. And no one ever let me forget that at the stroke of eighteen I was on my own."

"Without any help? Eighteen is still just a kid…"

"Not when you're in the system it isn't. Mature, immature, ready or not, you're an adult. There are some short-term transitional services and there's a little funding to get started, but basically, yes, you're on your own, without help. Unless you go on welfare and food stamps and go that route, but I hoped I wouldn't have to if I could be close to supporting myself when I graduated high school."

He took a deep breath and blew it out with puffed cheeks, his eyebrows arched over those blue eyes as if the image she was painting was baffling to him. "Eighteen and on your own without family as any kind of safety net."

"Without anything or anybody. If China and I hadn't become friends and stuck together neither of us would have had anyone at all to turn to or count on. We were in independent-living housing by the time we each turned eighteen, and because we hadn't dropped out of high school and were getting good grades, we were allowed to stay through graduation. But right after that we were out the door. And once we were, I had two more calls from my case worker to see how I was doing. China only had one and—"

"That was it?" he asked as if it was hard to fathom.

"That was it. *Because* I'd opted for trade school at thirteen I got to have some of my high school classes at the trade school—which was when I decided doing hair might be something I was good at—and it gave me a head start to finishing not long after graduation. And that's how I came to this. So, no, I didn't become a stylist just so I could be on the fringes of weddings and parties. But I'm glad it worked out that way and I think of it as a perk."

"And that's what you've done for how long?"

"I went to work a few months before I turned nineteen so…eleven years."

"Did you go to work at Beauty By Design at nineteen?"

She laughed again. "Uh…no, I worked in about a dozen different shops before that."

His eyebrows arched. "How come?"

She shrugged again. "I don't know. Someone I knew had a theory that not staying in one place for long was what I was used to because of the way I grew up—that I had a transient upbringing and that made me unstable." Mark's opinion. "But I think it's just hard to find a good fit."

"Is Beauty By Design a good fit?"

"I think so. For now. I've been with this shop for four years, which is the longest I've been in one place—that must mean something, right?" Which Mark had disregarded. "But I guess my résumé doesn't say much for my sticking power—twelve different salons in seven years…"

"You stuck with the same occupation, though," Dylan pointed out.

"That's true." And she wished it was an argument she'd thought to use before.

"What about you?" she asked then, for some reason feeling free to treat this as just any other conversation with any other person. "Did you say you do security?"

"I did and I do. I'm head of all of the security in every form for Camden Superstores and Camden Incorporated."

"Along with the security for your sister's wedding?" she asked, because his title seemed too elevated for something like that.

"Along with my sister's wedding."

"So while all the girls are here doing hair and nails and makeup and girlie things, and drinking and eating chocolate, you'll do what? Stand like a guard at the gate?"

It was his turn to laugh. Before his handsome face screwed up into a pained sort of expression. "Yeah, I'm afraid so."

"You couldn't delegate that job?"

He laughed again. "Ordinarily I would have. But I have some things to make up to my family and I've been out of the country for the last three months, so taking care of the wedding security myself and giving it all the personal touch is just sort of the way I think it needs to be done this time."

"You were out of the country for three months?"

"Working on the security issues in our European stores."

"Like, because of terrorist threats or something?"

"Well, those are everywhere these days. But that wasn't the primary purpose. Mostly I just refined systems, increased security against hacking, met with teams over there so I could get to know personnel and establish a presence..." He chuckled a bit wryly. "That all sounds really professional, doesn't it?" he asked with a humility she liked. "But the truth is that none of it was necessary. Mostly I was just getting away."

She wanted to ask from what but didn't feel free to. So instead she made a guess. "A three month paid vacation?"

"No, I worked the whole time. I wasn't really in the mood for anything else."

He also wasn't offering any details.

It felt as if she'd be overstepping her bounds to ask for those details so she decided to change the subject. "Wednesday will be pretty boring for you. And long— your sister's email said there will be her and her maid of honor and seven bridesmaids and maybe a couple of other family members not in the wedding party who might want to be done up for the occasion, so we'll be doing trials for them all?"

"That sounds about right. We're a big family. How would you like to meet them all tomorrow?"

That shocked her. "Meet them all?"

"We have Sunday dinner every week at GiGi's house. It's more than just family, though, everybody is free to bring friends or dates or whoever. We thought you might like to have a chance to get acquainted a little, see what you'll be dealing with in the way of hair and what-not so you can be thinking about it before Wednesday."

"Oh, no, it'll be fine," Abby said, because that sounded very daunting. "We do this all the time with all kinds of hair and skin types. We don't worry about what we're getting into because we've pretty much seen everything there is to see and can handle whatever we need to. And just because I said I like to look in on things from the sidelines doesn't mean I wish I was invited or anything…"

He shook his head. "My grandmother told me to invite you before you ever told me that stuff. She'd just like you to come, to meet you."

"I…it's…no… I wouldn't know what to do with my-self at something like that."

"A Sunday dinner? We eat, drink, talk—I haven't seen you eat or drink but I'm figuring you have some experience, and I know you can talk because, look at us, here we are, doing that. I promise you we're a group that's easy to be with. But if you want, you could bring China as your plus one, if that would make you more comfortable. And I won't leave your side for a minute."

Oh, that by-her-side thing again…

And there it was, making what he was proposing sound less intimidating.

But Sunday family dinner with the Camdens? With *all* of the Camdens? Even less intimidating was still plenty intimidating. It seemed like a bigger deal than a lot of the special occasion events she did. And if there was one thing she'd learned from peeking in or being on the sidelines, it was that foster care and group homes hadn't prepared her to fit in herself to the things she could style other people for.

"I wouldn't know what to wear." It had been hard enough trying to pick out the jeans and shirt she'd de-cided on tonight, just knowing she was going to see him. She didn't own anything as nice as the lightweight pale yellow crewneck sweater he had on with those jeans that probably cost what she paid in rent every month.

"GiGi's one rule is that there aren't any jeans al-lowed," he said into her near panic. "But we still dress casual and comfortable. Since we can't be sure how much longer the weather will be good we're doing one final barbecue of the season in GiGi's backyard. So to-morrow it'll be a lot of khakis and capri pants. Anything that isn't jeans will do fine." He tipped his chiseled chin in her direction cajolingly. "Come on...you'd be doing me a favor and giving me someone to hang out with."

"You have your whole family to hang out with."

"I kinda don't at the moment, actually."

That didn't make any sense. But once again he didn't explain himself.

He just said, "Come on...come with China and just meet everyone and indulge in some home cooking. Trust me, you'll have a good time. I'll make sure of it."

The idea was just so weird. She didn't hobnob with the kind of people she worked on.

She shook her head again. "I can't imagine—"

"I *promise* you it will be fun. Don't make me take no for an answer and have to go home a failure when you've made everything else work out so well for me..."

There was only the tiniest hint of mock pleading in his tone. It actually seemed as if he genuinely wanted her to go. And it came with such an engagingly crooked smile and a glint in those striking blue eyes.

It all made her waver—but not give in. Not quite yet. "I don't know..." she waffled. "I don't think—"

"Don't think, just say you'll come—with or without China."

"Oh, China would love it! She's very big on seeing how the other half lives." And this wasn't merely the other half—this was the most upper crust of the upper crust.

"Then do it for her."

Abby made a face. She was tempted—as she knew her friend would be—to see what a Camden family dinner might be like from the inside, but she was still really, really unsure about it.

"I'll come and pick the two of you up and bring you

home. You won't have to do a thing but enjoy yourselves, and GiGi will send you off with more leftovers than you'll be able to eat in a week. Come on…"

Maybe it was the third *come on* that was the charm. Or maybe it was sitting there with him for the past hour, talking to him as if he were nobody special even as she'd been marinating in just how hot he was and how comfortable she'd felt with him in spite of everything, but she heard herself say, "China and I were just going to maybe go to the zoo."

"You could do that earlier in the day—we start appetizers at five, dinner is at six, so I'd pick you up at around four-thirty."

Dylan took his phone out of his pocket. "Tell me China's phone number—I'll call her right now and invite her, too. She'll make you say that yes, you'll both come."

"Nooo…you wouldn't have to do that…" she demurred, knowing China needed to hear all of this from her or she wouldn't believe it at all.

"So you'll just say yes on your own?"

"I suppose it wouldn't do any harm to know what we'll be working with on Wednesday, since we've never met the bride and it's such a big wedding party."

"Right!"

"But aren't we…like…the *help* or the employees or the service providers or…you know, something that shouldn't really be *guests*?" she asked, doubting her decision even as she'd made it.

"We don't see things that way. Tomorrow you'll meet Margaret and Louie Haliburton. They've been with GiGi since the Dark Ages, on the payroll as house staff, but they're her best friends and they helped her raise us all so you can consider them *our* foster family."

He'd lost her—his grandmother had raised him with the help of the...help?

Before she could ask him to explain, he said, "Say I can count on you."

It was a command as he looked intently into her eyes with those devastatingly blue ones of his. And they somehow mesmerized her for a moment, drawing her out of herself, to him.

He was clean shaven again...as if he planned to be kissed. Or to be doing the kissing.

She didn't know why that popped into her head, but it did.

And for no conceivable reason she was suddenly imagining him leaning forward and kissing her...

Until it struck her that she'd gone out of her mind.

Because what else could explain thinking of kissing him? Him, of all people—a Camden!

She mentally shook herself back into the real world, and knew she probably should firmly decline his invitation, after all.

And even if she'd come too far for that, she certainly shouldn't *ever* be thinking about kissing him!

"Say it," he demanded.

Say what? she wondered before she recalled that he wanted her to tell him he could count on her for dinner the next night.

Could he count on her?

For haircuts. For hairstyles. But for anything else? He'd likely be disappointed.

But despite thinking that, she said, "Okay, but it might be the dumbest idea you've ever had."

He grinned. So charmingly.

"Oh, Abby, this is so far from being that!" he said.

Then he got down from the pedicure station and held

out his hand to her to help her down, too. "I'll let you get home—you worked all day and here I've kept you working tonight."

Nothing about tonight had felt like work.

But she didn't say that.

And without thinking about it, she slipped her hand into his.

Why, she didn't know. It wasn't as if she needed the aid. And she definitely shouldn't have done it, because the minute her hand was nestled in his big, warm one, it felt like heaven.

Forbidden heaven because he was a client and a Camden, and she reminded herself that she couldn't possibly be more out of her depth than she was with him.

So she retracted her hand the very second her feet were on the floor and said, "You can go ahead. I need to do a couple of things to get ready for Wednesday."

It was a bold-faced lie. But she was afraid if she walked out with him she might lapse into thinking about kissing him again and she couldn't risk it.

He didn't question her, though. He merely headed for the shop door.

"Four-thirty tomorrow," he repeated. "Text me your address and I'll bring a car with no dents and more than two seats."

That confused her, too. But she felt so dazed by then that she thought it might have been perfectly clear to someone else.

She only nodded and watched him open the door.

As he went through it he cast her one last glance over his shoulder. He had the kind of smile on his face that said he liked what he saw when he caught that final sight of her. Then he pulled the door closed after himself and he was gone.

And that was when Abby deflated. Swallowed hard. And wondered if she'd stepped into some other world or something.

Because somehow she didn't feel as though she was still in her own.

Chapter Four

Abby didn't know why she didn't have the same attitude toward the Camden Sunday dinner that China had.

"Woo-hoo! Partying with the rich! Better than the zoo!"

That had been China's response to the invitation.

But, for some reason, the upcoming event carried more weight for Abby.

She couldn't decide what to wear and tried on half the clothes in her closet before finally choosing a red-and-white cap-sleeved sundress that was snug through the top and connected by a high, banded waist to a flowy knee-length skirt.

She only owned one pair of dressy sandals so there was no other option in footwear, but she redid her hair three times—all up, partially pulled back, all pulled back—before China convinced her to just let it fall freely into its own full, natural curls around her shoulders.

She also let China do her makeup—not the more elab-

orate version that China did on herself, which sported
her trademark sultry eyes, but a natural look that still
managed to be slightly more party-like than usual. Then
she made China tone that down some because she was
afraid it was *too* party-like.

And even after she was mostly satisfied, she was
still such a bundle of nerves that it was palpable when
she and China went out onto the old Victorian house's
wraparound front porch to wait for Dylan.

"This is only a lark," China reminded her. "It doesn't
make any difference what they think of us or whether
they like us or they don't."

Abby was haunted for a split second by the mental
image of Dylan in response to that and the strong sense
that it *did* make a difference. At least to her.

But then she shoved it away.

Because, no, it didn't make any difference whether
he liked her or not. Even if she hadn't been able to stop
thinking about him for more than five minutes since
she'd watched him walk out the door last night. She'd
had him in mind the whole time she was getting ready
for this barbecue today.

"It just seems weird," she told her friend. "Should
I be mad at these people or hate them or something?
I mean, if their family hadn't been hardnosed to their
employees and sent Gus Glassman to take care of their
problems he wouldn't have gone to jail and I would have
grown up with a father. Now here I am going to their
house for a barbecue as if it's some kind of reunion. Is
that something I should be doing?"

"Like, are you showing some kind of disloyalty if you
do?" China shrugged elaborately. "I don't know, Ab. Do
you *feel* like a rat for doing it?"

She felt a lot of things. Mostly awkward and out of her depth.

Yes, she'd been in any number of upper-class homes prepping upper-class brides who were willing to pay extra for the special occasions group to go to them, but she'd never been in one of them to *attend* a party and she was worried she might do something clumsy or awkward or cloddish.

She was uncomfortable with the thought of rubbing shoulders with people like the Camdens in a completely social situation and not within her own bailiwick where she knew exactly what to do and what her role was.

But did she feel like a rat—as China put it? Or somehow disloyal?

No, when she analyzed her feelings, she couldn't say she felt either of those things. Maybe because her relationship to Gus still didn't feel quite real. She didn't feel as if he was a part of her, so when she tried to figure out what he would have wanted, what he would have felt about her accepting this invitation…she couldn't even make a decent guess. He might have been her father, but she didn't know him. Not well enough to know how he'd have thought or felt, anyway.

But what she also felt—hiding underneath all the tension and compounding her confusion—was a flicker of China's level of excitement and an eagerness that was pressing her forward. Except that where China's enthusiasm was all for the event and the food and the opportunity to be a guest, Abby's excitement and eagerness seemed to be completely centered around seeing Dylan again.

So, rather than answer her friend's question about what she was feeling she repeated, "It just seems weird."

"Sure. The whole thing is weird. But I think things

happen for a reason. You have to play them out to see where they lead, because where they lead is the reason."

Abby laughed. "You think the guy who was supposedly my father killed someone and abandoned me to grow up in foster care just so I could end up eating ribs with rich people?"

"Oh, I hope there'll be ribs! I love ribs!" China rhapsodized before she said, "You've just gotta let it play out, Ab. See where it goes."

But where letting-things-play-out went at that moment, when a big black SUV pulled up to the curb in front of them with Dylan behind the wheel, made her heart race. It made her have to fight the urge to rush to the car. It made the sun suddenly seem brighter and all of her stress take an instant backseat to a level of joy that she'd never experienced before, blossoming now at just the sight of him again.

And somehow she didn't think *that* was where anything was supposed to go.

"You've got that look with her, Dylan—don't you think you ought to keep it cool?"

"I'm cool, Cade. I'm perfectly chill. I just don't want Abby to feel like a fish out of water with us all so I'm staying close. We're a lot for her to deal with."

Abby didn't mean to overhear what was being said between Dylan and the man named Cade, whom she thought was one of Dylan's cousins. But Dylan had taken her inside to wash her hands in the bathroom, and he'd assured her that he'd wait for her in the kitchen. So the kitchen was where she'd headed after the handwashing and there they were.

Not wanting to eavesdrop or interrupt, she retraced

her steps and returned to the bathroom to give them a few minutes.

And while she was doing that, she started to think about what she'd overheard.

Cade had sounded a little alarmed, maybe a little miffed, and there was a warning note in his voice when he'd said Dylan needed to *keep it cool.*

If Dylan's answer hadn't been about her she might have thought the subject was something else. Because there did seem to be some tension among the Camdens when it came to Dylan.

But Dylan's answer *had* been about her, so it was her they were talking about.

Her, who he needed to *keep it cool* with.

Was it *because* she was, as Dylan had said, a fish out of water? And what did that mean? Was he saying that she was bound to feel out of place because she didn't belong—as in, wasn't good enough?

Certainly she had experience being considered unworthy, so that seemed like the likeliest meaning to her. And it wasn't as if it came as a surprise. She *was* a fish out of water here, with these people.

The Tudor-style house was bigger than any she'd ever been in before. So big she wasn't sure she could have found the bathroom without Dylan's help.

And the Camdens? All of them were smart and great-looking and accomplished, and even though they were down-to-earth people and treated her and China with warmth and kindness, going out of their way to make them feel at home and a part of everything, she and China were still…well…she and China.

And regardless of what kind of spin was put on it, they *were* fish out of water here. There was just no denying it.

So maybe it was good to be reminded of it, she

thought. Especially when they'd all made her feel so at home that it was easy to lose sight of it.

Especially when it had been so nice—and so comfortable—having Dylan by her side the whole evening, making her forget that she *was* out of her depth with him.

Especially when, as the evening had progressed, she'd begun to feel like his date.

And that was a bad thing to have slipped into, she realized. She wasn't here on a date with him. She wasn't meeting the family of someone she was involved with. This wasn't anything like that.

This was sort of a job interview combined with the Camdens' guilty consciences, and that was it. They seemed like genuinely nice people, but when the wedding was over and her stylist services were no longer needed, when the lockbox Gus Glassman had left was found and Dylan had helped her explore her heritage, it would be The End, Duty Done, Have A Nice Life. And she'd never see or hear from any of these people— including Dylan—again.

And that was so, so, so important for her to remember, she told herself as she realized that she'd gone from being a nervous wreck about tonight to feeling *too* comfortable.

No good could come of that.

No good had come of it with Mark and she'd learned her lesson.

And she wasn't dumb enough to have to learn it again, on an even larger scale.

She'd been in the bathroom long enough and really needed to return to the kitchen before someone came to check on her. So she opened the door and made sure it gently hit the wall to alert whoever was in the kitchen that she was coming out.

But what look did Dylan have for her?

That question struck her only as she made her second approach to the kitchen where Dylan was now alone.

He spotted her the minute she got to the entrance and there was an immediate smile, a sort of perking up, and maybe a hint of something that made it seem as if he was glad to see her—the way she'd been glad to see him when he'd picked her up today.

And, yes, maybe it did have a little something extra in it that it shouldn't have had.

But regardless of why that alarmed his family enough to warn him about it, it was the warm-honey feeling that it made course through Abby that alarmed her...

"You were right—it will take us a week to eat all these leftovers," Abby said to Dylan as she tried to fasten her seatbelt behind the containers on her lap.

She and Dylan were back in his SUV, parked near an enormous fountain that was at the center of the cobbled, circular driveway outside of his grandmother's house.

It was shortly before nine o'clock. China had hit it off with another guest at the Camdens' Sunday dinner, and since she wasn't scheduled to work until afternoon on Monday, she'd agreed to go with him for a drink. Abby and Dylan had been asked to go along but Abby was slated to open Beauty By Design first thing in the morning and had used that as her excuse to decline.

Because going for a drink with Dylan, China and China's impromptu date really would have made her feel as if she was on a date of her own with Dylan. And putting herself in that position seemed like a mistake.

"GiGi can't let anyone go away empty-handed," Dylan said in response.

He was in the driver's seat, and in order to set down

his own containers he reached around Abby's seat to put them on the floor behind her.

He didn't come too close in order to accomplish that, but close enough to give her a whiff of that clean-smelling cologne he wore. And although she told herself she was imagining it, Abby thought she could feel a heady heat coming from him that her own body seemed drawn to. To the extent that it took some effort to keep herself still rather than leaning ever so slightly toward him the way she wanted to.

Then he sat up straight, and there was the distance of the console between them again.

Not really a safe distance, but some distance, at least. She relaxed again.

He started the engine, and as they followed the drive around and out to the street he said, "Did I make that painless enough for you?"

It took a moment to realize he was talking about the evening they'd just spent with his family.

It had taken some time for her to get over her nerves when she'd first arrived, and then she'd overheard his cousin reminding him that she wasn't good enough for him. Neither of those things were totally pain free, but she wasn't going to tell him about them so instead she said, "On the whole, pretty painless, yeah. Thank you."

"I'm just glad you came. This was the first Sunday dinner since I got back from Europe that was almost painless for me, too, and that's all because I was there with the woman of the hour."

Everyone whose hair she would be doing on Wednesday had wanted to talk to her about it, so she knew what he meant about her being the woman of the hour. As for it being almost painless for him, she still had no clue what was going on between him and his family but it was clear there was some tension there. She could see where having her as a buffer had probably made it easier for him.

And that was likely the real reason he hadn't left her side, she told herself to make absolutely sure that she didn't lapse into believing there was any other reason—for instance that he'd *wanted* to be with her.

"Your family is great," she declared then. "You're lucky to have them." Regardless of whatever was amiss at the moment. "It's bigger than the imaginary family I had as a kid, but just about as perfect."

"You had an imaginary family?" he asked.

"Oh, sure. For years and years when I was little. Mother, father, grandparents, two imaginary sisters and two imaginary brothers. And there was also an imaginary big dog and an imaginary little dog."

"No cats?" he asked, laughing.

"I'm allergic to those."

He laughed again. "Even imaginary ones?"

Abby smiled and chastised him. "How realistic would it have seemed if I didn't have the allergy there, too?"

"Good point," he agreed.

She glanced over at him, craving the sight of him as if she'd gone months rather than minutes without it.

He was wearing khaki slacks and a dark green sport shirt that did nothing for his eyes and wasn't a color she would ever put him in. And yet she still thought he looked amazing.

Searching for something else to talk about as he drove through the streets of Cherry Creek, she said, "I really liked Margaret and Louie, too. I see what you mean now about how even though they work for your grandmother, they are still sort of your foster family, too."

"Yep."

"And did I hear you right? Did you say they helped

your grandmother raise you all? Because I didn't really think at the time where your parents might have been in that but today—"

"There weren't any parents there," he finished for her. "Because when I was eight all the adults in my family—except for GiGi and H.J.—"

"Your great-grandfather, the guy who started it all."

"Right. All the rest of the adults in my family were killed in a plane crash."

He went on to tell her that GiGi had denied herself the family vacation to care for her father-in-law when he'd hurt his back, sparing the two of them, who would otherwise have been lost, too.

"Oh! I didn't know. I'm sorry!"

"It was a long time ago." He deflected her condolences.

"I shouldn't have asked."

"It's really okay. It was too long ago to be a sore spot," he answered.

"But, still, that's the kind of story that got kids I knew into foster care. You were orphaned."

"We were lucky. We had GiGi. And H.J. And Margaret and Louie. They moved us all into GiGi's house, and that's where I grew up from eight years old on—I'm betting that doesn't compare to foster homes."

"But you still grew up without any parents," she mused, stunned to have learned that about him. "It just never occurred to me that something bad—especially *that* bad—could have happened to you. To your family…"

He took a deep, steeling breath, as if he needed it even to think about the past. "Money doesn't protect you from tragedy," he said. "And that was definitely a tragedy. But at least we had each other."

She knew he was referring to her being alone in the

world. But she also recognized that the difference in their situations didn't make his any less difficult for him.

"What was the worst part for you?" she asked, to let him know that she understood what he must have gone through.

"I hated Mother's Day and Father's Day," he said with a slight chuckle, as if that wasn't really a monumental enough thing to be the worst part. "Especially in elementary school when we'd have to make cards— it would raise questions I didn't want to answer when I made them for my grandmother and Margaret or for my great-grandfather and Louie instead."

So he'd gone through some of what she had.

"I know. Me, too," she said, stunned that they had this—of all things—in common when she'd been so sure that he'd come from just the kind of family she'd wished for.

Then she said, "I remember things from when I was eight—a few anyway—so you must have some memories of your parents."

"Some, yeah," he admitted. "I remember enough to have carried with me a sense of them, I guess. I remember when we were all together in our own house, the last Christmas when I got my first two-wheel bike, and my dad worked with me until we could take the training wheels off. I remember some birthdays—with six kids, how could I not? I remember going as a family to GiGi's for Sunday dinner—"

"Even then?"

"Always."

"And you must remember what it was like to lose them," she said softly as he drove out of downtown, feeling sympathy for the eight-year-old Dylan for hav-

ing endured something she'd gone through at too young
an age to clearly recall.

"*That* I remember pretty well, yeah," he answered
somberly. "For the vacation my brothers and sisters and
I were staying at home with our nanny, and our cousins
were staying at their house with theirs. So I remember
when we were all picked up suddenly and brought to
GiGi's house—all of us and all of the cousins. When
GiGi and H.J. and Margaret and Louie sat us together
in the living room and told us what had happened. It
didn't seem real at first—although I couldn't figure out
why the four of them would play such a mean trick on
us. And then there was the funeral—five coffins. I kept
counting them over and over… I guess that's weird," he
said with a humorless little laugh and a glance at her.

Abby shrugged. "You were a kid. It just seems like
something you did to get you through it."

"Yeah, I suppose that's true," he agreed.

Abby was still watching him, studying his profile,
and she saw a muscle flex and unflex in his jaw as he
seemed to relive some of that time.

"You must have been sad after that," she said. "Kids
who came into foster care after the deaths of parents
usually cried a lot, through the night… I always felt so
bad for them. For me, being in foster care, not having
parents, was just the way it had always been. I didn't remember anything else. But kids who remembered having parents really suffered."

"We were all sad," Dylan said. "GiGi had lost her husband, her sons, both daughters-in-law. Even H.J.—I'd
never seen him look the way he did then, and that was
scary to me as a kid. Even though he was in his eighties,
he was still a big man, and strong. But after the plane
crash… I don't know, he looked…smaller. Defeated. For

a while. Then he went back into action, running the business again at eighty-eight—"

"That old?"

"Yep. But knowing his own limitations, he went back mainly to put together a board of directors that he could trust to run things, making it clear that they were only in place until we all grew up and could take over. At home he started training us for that, to make sure we all knew running the business was going to be our job." He shrugged. "And that's what we did."

"Whether you wanted to or not?" she asked, wondering if—for entirely different reasons—she also wasn't the only one of them not to have had many options about the path her adult life had taken.

"Yeah, whether we wanted to or not. But Camden Incorporated is a big organization. There's been a lot of room for each of us to find our own niche, just within the company. But we all grew up knowing it was our responsibility to carry on the family business, that it was ours to operate, to keep going—there was no wiggle-room there."

"Were you okay with that?"

"I was. I am. And I haven't heard any complaints from anyone else. And we all work pretty well together—even lately when there's been some other stuff going on, we still haven't had trouble agreeing on business things."

They'd reached her apartment and he parked in front, turning off his engine.

That told her he didn't intend for her to just jump out and she thought he was merely going to be gentlemanly and walk her to the door.

But when he unfastened his seatbelt he didn't reach for the door handle. He pivoted toward her, rested an arm across the top of her seat and smiled. "I didn't mean for this to turn glum," he said.

What he'd said couldn't compare to some of the glum stories she'd encountered, but she didn't tell him that.

And since he didn't seem to be in any hurry for this night to end yet, she said, "So, you were orphaned—sort of like me—and raised to know you had to work in the family business. But what were you like as a boy? Were you the family troublemaker?"

He laughed. "Why? Because I'm in trouble now?"

She arched her eyebrows in a way that said *maybe,* even though she still didn't know why he was in trouble.

"No, I was not the family troublemaker," he said as if she was far off base. "But I guess I did have an early start in security, now that I think about it. I was always pretty protective of the girls, and when it came to the guys, a lot of the time I somehow ended up involved in everybody else's fights as backup. Outside of the family, anyway. Which means I went home with a lot of black eyes from fights that had nothing to do with me."

"So were all your scrapes from somebody else's fights? Did you toe the line completely yourself?"

He grinned in a way that put just a touch of devilishness into his eyes. "I said I wasn't the family troublemaker. But I wasn't the family saint, either. Some of the scrapes were my own, too. Boys will be boys, you know..."

"So how did you go from protecting your family and helping them fight their battles, to ticking them all off?" she ventured, dying to know what he could possibly have done to aggravate such a close-knit group.

He looked steadily at her. "I thought I was protecting and standing up for someone else—"

"*Against* your family?" she blurted out, because she

couldn't fathom doing anything to alienate a family like that if it was hers.

"Let's say I was defending someone who was in *conflict* with my family…it was all just confused and misleading and a mess, and now I'm on the naughty list for it. But I'm working on things. It's not a lost cause. I'll get forgiveness eventually."

It must be nice to be so secure in his position that he knew that would happen. That was something Abby had never had any experience with.

But she didn't say that. And she didn't feel as if she could ask him any more, even though she really wanted to.

Then, as if to fill the silence before she could press him any further, he smiled a crooked smile and said, "And pulling off the coup of getting you for the wedding is helping me make strides in the direction of forgiveness."

"So you're using me," she challenged him.

He scrunched up that handsome face as if she'd hit him. "Ooh, no! I'm just trying to balance things—on your side I'm trying to give you some business and some great word-of-mouth to add to your already shining reputation, along with helping you find out about your family history. On the other side, I'm trying to fix one of the glitches with my sister's wedding. Am I hoping to come out at the end in a better light with the family myself? Yes. But I'm gonna do my damnedest to make sure there are more benefits for you than for anyone, and some for my family, too, so everybody comes out ahead. Please don't tell me any of that makes you feel *used*…"

She couldn't suppress a grin at the lengthy explanation that simple comment had elicited. "It's okay. I'm not worried that you're using me. I was just giving you a hard time."

"Don't do that to me. I've already got enough people angry with me," he beseeched.

She understood that because she'd seen him get a few cold shoulders today.

"Okay," she said, as if she were conceding to something. "You have my permission to ride my coattails if you need to."

He laughed. "I do, and thank you," he said jokingly. "And I definitely like you thinking you're doing me a favor better than thinking that I'm *using* you."

"Oh, I like that better, too," she said as if it were a revelation.

He was smiling warmly at her, studying her in a way that seemed as if he was again finding things in her that he hadn't expected to find, things he liked.

And she so liked him looking at her that way…

Which was how they sat for a moment—a moment when thoughts of kissing came into her head again—before he raised his chin as if dragging himself out of his own thoughts and said, "You have an early morning tomorrow and here I am holding you up. Wait there and I'll come around and help you carry all those containers up to your door."

Abby nodded and he turned to get out.

While he came around to her side she unfastened her seatbelt and got her purse onto her shoulder so she was ready when he opened her door to hand him some of the containers.

Neither of them said anything until they reached the old house's porch.

"I'm upstairs, China is right across the hall," she explained.

"Then let me go up with you to carry these," he offered.

She braced the food containers she was carrying against the front of her and opened the door, leading him through what the landlady called the vestibule and up the flight of carpeted stairs to the second floor.

"Let me unlock my door and then I'll take those containers back from you," Abby said. "China said she wouldn't be late but this stuff should probably go in my refrigerator, just in case. I can give her her share tomorrow."

"Sure," he agreed, waiting patiently while she put the key in the lock and then pushed open her door just barely, because she didn't want him to see the mess she'd left trying to decide what to wear.

"Go ahead and stack them on these," she suggested, holding out her containers to accept his.

He stepped close to set them down but once he had he didn't move back again. He stayed where he was, only inches from her.

And he was looking at her intently once more, with those blue eyes full of something she couldn't explain, but something that seemed—and felt—warm and admiring.

"Thanks for coming tonight," he said then, his voice deeper, quieter, as if for her ears alone.

"Thanks for inviting us. It was fun."

"I hope so," he said, still scanning her face, her eyes, her mouth…

And suddenly she was fairly certain that she wasn't the only one of them thinking about kissing, that he was, too.

That he might even be leaning slightly forward.

That he might even do it…

And even as everything in her shouted warnings that it wasn't something she should let happen, her chin tilted a fraction of an inch all on its own to make it easier for him.

But after a moment he yanked his head back as if his better judgment had finally kicked in, and he stepped away.

"We've narrowed down the stores where Gus Glassman might have hidden the lockbox," he said then. "As soon as we find it I'll let you know. If that isn't before Wednesday then I guess I'll just see you at the trial run for the wedding."

Abby nodded once more. "Okay," she said softly.

Then she again raised her chin, not in an invitation but with pride, to let him know she didn't care that he hadn't gone through with a kiss.

Whether or not that was how he read it, he said goodnight and headed back down the stairs.

Abby slipped into her apartment and closed the door behind her, knowing even as she did that that last bit of cheekiness had been nothing but a show.

Because, despite being convinced that no kissing should now or ever pass between them, she still cared that he might have been tempted to do it but had stopped when he'd recalled his cousin's warning.

The warning that had to mean Cade thought she wasn't good enough for Dylan.

And if he hadn't kissed her because he thought she wasn't good enough for him, she not only cared, she cared a lot more than she wished she did.

Chapter Five

"What did you say this man's name is?" Abby asked Dylan.

He'd called on Monday night to tell her that the lockbox had been found and that he'd also tracked down a former employee who had worked closely with her father, seemed to know him fairly well and was willing to talk with them about him.

Abby's last appointment on Tuesday was at three in the afternoon. Dylan had said he could get away from work at four and would pick her up shortly after that in order for them to meet with Gus's old acquaintance. That was what they were on their way to do now. Afterward they were going to pick up the lockbox that was being held for them at the store.

"Marty Sorensen is the guy's name," Dylan answered as he got on the highway in the direction of Aurora.

"And how did he know Gus? Did he do the same kind of things for your family?"

She was looking at Dylan in profile as he drove, so she saw the frown that gave her an answer before he said, "I'm pretty sure he did. There seems to be kind of a split between people who worked straight-up security for us and…"

"The enforcers," Abby supplied.

"Yeah," he conceded. "When I called around to other people on the security roster at the time they were…well, let's say they didn't want to talk about Gus Glassman. A couple of them said if I wanted to know anything about him I should talk to *his crew*—Marty Sorensen or some other guys whose names seemed to bring out the same attitude in people."

"A negative one?" Abby guessed.

"Not a positive one, that's for sure," Dylan said somewhat under his breath.

"The security personnel who weren't the boss's bullies didn't want to be connected to the boss's bullies," she suggested, once more not thrilled to hear that her father seemed to have also been the kind of person she'd avoided in foster and group homes.

"That's the impression I got," Dylan confirmed. "Of all the names I was given of other members of his group, I could only reach two of them. And the first guy said he'd worked with Gus but didn't know him well enough to talk about him—"

"Or he didn't want to admit to it," Abby muttered.

"But Marty Sorensen actually seemed happy to tell us anything we wanted to know and invited us over to his place to do it."

"Did he seem…you know…like a roughneck? Are you sure we should be going to his house? Maybe it would be better to meet him in a public place," Abby said, thinking that possibly they should practice more caution.

Dylan took his eyes off the road long enough to cast her a smile. "When they were working together, Marty was old enough to be Gus's father. Now the guy is in his eighties and it's his apartment in an assisted-living facility that we're going to. Even if he used to be a *roughneck* I think I can keep him in line if I need to." He laughed as he added, "I don't know exactly what these guys were like in their prime, but I'm reasonably sure we aren't in any danger from Marty Sorensen this afternoon."

"Maybe I'm not, but he could pull out a gun and hold you for ransom," she said as a comeback to his amusement.

"Then *you'll* have to save *me*," he said.

"Oh, you're out of luck—I'm not taking a bullet for you," she joked even as she drank in the sight of him.

She'd had time to run home and change from her work clothes into a pair of black capris and a black tank top that she wore under a meant-to-be-seen-through sheer white shirt decorated with embroidered flowers.

But he was still wearing part of what she assumed was a work suit—gray slacks with only a faint dove gray stripe to them, and a dove-gray dress shirt with the collar button open and the sleeves now rolled to mid-forearm, exposing thick wrists that—for some strange reason—she really liked the look of.

He was cleanly shaven, though, and he smelled great so he must have done that much sprucing up at his office. And Abby wished it didn't feel so good to be with him again and that she didn't find it quite as easy as she did to talk to him, to joke around with him, to tease him, to be herself with him.

The assisted-living facility was right off the highway and there was ample parking. Once they found the unit number Dylan parked directly in front of it.

There were lawn chairs on the small porch that went with every apartment and Dylan nodded at them. "It's a nice day, would you feel better if we got him to sit outside with us?"

"No, I'll try to keep you safe inside," she said with mock resignation.

"Thanks, that makes me feel so much better," he countered with another laugh.

Abby didn't wait for him to come around to her side of the SUV—the same SUV she'd ridden in with him to Sunday dinner.

She met him at the curb and they walked side by side to the unit's door. For some reason, along the way she had the oddest desire for him to reach for her hand to hold. It made no sense. She could only account for it as her wanting comfort before meeting some former thug who had known her apparently-also-thuggish father.

But holding hands certainly wasn't going to happen, and feeling the need to do something with hers, she put them in her pants pockets.

Dylan knocked on the door. Just a few moments later, it opened and all of her attention went to the elderly man standing there.

He was not quite as tall as Dylan, with a full head of snow-white hair and a congenial but craggy and vastly wrinkled face that had likely never been considered handsome. Where there once must have been muscle, he was now only skin and bones that left his clothes— khaki-green trousers and a plaid flannel shirt—hanging loosely on him. There was nothing at all intimidating about him.

"Marty?" Dylan asked.

"You must be Mr. Camden," the old man responded respectfully.

"Dylan, please," Dylan amended, sounding respectful himself and as if he was uncomfortable with the elderly man's deference. "And this is Abby Crane—Gus Glassman's daughter."

"I knew it!" Marty Sorensen said. "You're the spittin' image of your momma! Same hair and those eyes—big and dark. I thought she might be Eye-talian but Gus said no, didn't I see how fair of skin she was? Irish through and through. A beauty, though! And that's alive in you, for sure!" The elderly man stepped out of the doorway and said, "Come on in."

Abby had no idea why she looked to Dylan but he was watching her and raised his eyebrows as if leaving it up to her whether she accepted the invitation or ran the other way.

Part of her *wanted* to run the other way, a little afraid somehow of learning whatever it was that Dylan had uncovered for her.

Then he gave a slight nod toward the inside of the apartment and she could have sworn he was telling her it was all right. That everything would be all right.

And from that she found the courage to go in, with Dylan close enough behind her that she could still feel his presence—something she appreciated. And, strangely enough for someone accustomed to going through her life basically alone, something she felt a need for all of a sudden.

After asking if he could get them something to eat or drink—and Abby and Dylan assuring the older man that they were fine—the three of them sat in the apartment's tiny living room. Dylan and Abby took the love seat they were motioned to, and Marty Sorensen gingerly lowered himself into an old lounger that seemed held together by strips of silver duct tape.

"I can't believe a real live Camden is here in my house," Marty Sorensen said then, sounding honored. "H.J. Camden's boy—"

"Actually, H.J. was my great-grandfather," Dylan said.

"Fine man, that Mr. Camden. But hard as nails," Marty Sorensen proclaimed.

"He was important to me. Good to me," Dylan said without confirming or denying the type of person his great-grandfather had been.

"And young Gus!" the elderly man said then, switching his attention to Abby. "You were the apple of that boy's eye! You and your momma while he had her. Only met her once, a few weeks before you were born—they got married just the two of them at the courthouse without any fuss so I wasn't invited to that and then…well. I think he was probably right to keep his sweet young wife and his work separate. But from what I heard from him, those two were happy as clams together. Young Gus said they were lucky to have each other, both of them alone in the world—"

"Neither of them had any family?" Dylan asked.

"Not a one. The way Gus told it," Marty went from answering Dylan to talking to Abby again, "your momma was born to people too old to have kids—she was a change-of-life baby. They'd died someways or another before she even met Gus and she didn't have any other family. Young Gus's folks were killed together in some kind of boating accident when he was barely seventeen. He was on his own from then—had to quit school and get work to live. He had kind of a chip on his shoulder by the time he came to work for the Camdens—life had knocked him around pretty good. I think he was 'bout twenty-three or-four when Mr. H.J. put him with us—

probably because he was a big galoot of a kid and that chip on his shoulder came in handy for the kind of jobs we were called on to do."

The elderly man cleared his throat, apparently stopping himself from going into detail about those jobs.

When he went on it was in a better direction. "Young Gus got plenty happy when he met your momma, though. He'd say he felt like he'd struck gold in her. Then in you. Never saw any man who loved his wife and baby like he did. Then he lost that momma of yours. It was a shame for that poor boy."

"How did he…lose her?" Abby asked.

"She was hit by a car walkin' to church of all things. You were…oh, just a little baby—a few months old. Gus was home with you, both of you sick that Sunday, or you might all have been goners. I guess she went to early services so she could get home to take care of the both of you and some guy still drunk from a bender the night before just ran her over—"

The elderly man caught himself and said, "Oh, maybe I should remember who I'm talkin' to." He was glancing at Dylan when he said that and Abby wondered if Dylan had given him some kind of signal to tone it down.

"That boy was in bad shape after that, I'll tell you," Marty said then. "It was you, pretty missy, that got him by, but just barely. *Me and my girl*—that's what he'd say, sobbin' like a baby. *I gotta keep goin' even if it's just me and my girl left.* Tore me up to see it."

Another solemn shake of the old man's head.

"Maybe that's how things went as bad as they did that day with that supervisor," Marty muttered more to himself than to either of them.

"The chip came back on Gus's shoulder?" Dylan

guessed, as if there were some things he wanted to know for himself.

"It was like there was two of him then," the elderly man said. "On the one hand he'd take out the picture of you that he always carried in his shirt pocket," he said to Abby, "and he'd smile and touch your face like it was you right there with him—all gentle and soft-eyed." Back to Dylan he said, "But yeah, on the job, sometimes there was maybe more temper to him than there should have been after losin' that wife of his. Shorter fuse, you know? We just thought it helped to get the job done, but then—" More head shaking.

"Were you with Gus when the supervisor was killed?" Dylan inquired.

"I was. That supervisor was a hothead himself. He jumped us. Came at us from behind, surprised us before we'd even had words with him. Had a pipe. Knocked me to the ground. I was tryin' to get my bearings again when he went for Gus. But that was when it went real bad. Nothin' I could do, half blacked out on the floor, and the next thing I knew...well, the whole thing'd gone south."

Marty Sorensen spoke to Abby again then. "I said that at Gus's trial—that the supervisor came at us first. But he was a scrawny fella, that supervisor. A lot smaller than Gus. And the two factory workers who'd seen it said Gus'd knocked the pipe out of the supervisor's hands early on in the fight and still went on givin' him a beat-down anyways. Till the supervisor hit his head and...well, the supervisor was pretty beat up—besides bein' dead—so I guess the jury figured Gus'd gone too far, even though he weren't the one to start the fight. Hated to see it. That boy didn't deserve to go to prison."

"What happened after the sentencing?" Dylan said

then. "I mean, you knew Gus had a little girl and no family to leave her with—"

"Mr. H.J. sent me away from here soon as I'd testified. Sent me to London, England," Marty said proudly. "To look after things that were stirred up with the opening of a Camdens there—that Harrods place didn't like it nohow. I barely got word what the jury had said 'bout poor Gus. I figured he must've found somebody to take that little girl of his. A friend or somebody." Those answers had gone to Dylan. But to Abby he said, "What did he do with you?"

Abby felt Dylan flinch beside her and he did reach for her hand then, squeezing it for only a split second before letting it go, as if offering support against the impact of the elderly man's bluntness.

She answered the question and the old man flinched then, too. "Oh…well…that couldn'ta been good."

"It wasn't," Dylan confirmed. "Until now she hasn't even known who Gus Glassman was, let alone that he was her father or anything about her mother or…anything."

"I'm sorry," the elderly man said. "I didn't think past… I just went on doin' what I was told, goin' where I was sent. It was the job, you know? I couldn'ta done anything for you anyways, an old bachelor like me, livin' in one room with a hot plate even before I went to London."

"I'm sure that's true," Abby said kindly, certain that it was. Even if Gus had persuaded Marty to take her, he probably wouldn't have passed muster getting approved as a foster parent. She would have ended up in the system, anyway.

"I'll tell you, though, that boy was crazy about you." The elderly man reverted to assuring her of that. "The sun rose and set in your momma, and then still in you even after losin' her. Had to have killed him inside to leave you…"

"I'm sure it did," Dylan contributed.

They meant well. Abby knew that. But she was numb. Or dazed, maybe. And still what she was hearing merely seemed like more words, a story, not anything that felt real or personally connected to her.

"That's about all I know," Marty said then. "It was a bad thing that happened all the way around but before that, young Gus got a little happiness with you and your momma, and I guess that's somethin'. For him, anyways. For you—"

"The information was what we wanted," Dylan said, as if he didn't want Abby reminded any more than she already had been about how things had turned out for her.

Or maybe it was something he didn't want to think about himself.

He wouldn't have been the first man she'd met who felt that way.

Then to her, he said, "Is there anything else you want to know, Abby?"

"I don't know what else to ask," she answered.

"Then maybe we should go."

"You can call me if there's anything else that you think of. I pretty much told you all I know—we just worked together, me and young Gus. But could be I'd have an answer if there was something else you thought of."

"We appreciate that," Dylan told him. "And thanks for seeing us today. For what you did tell us."

Dylan took a business card out of his pocket and handed it to the elderly man. "If there's anything I can do for you, let me know." He pointed his chin at the ragged lounger as he and Abby stood. "A new chair for starters—on the house—if you want one."

The old man grinned. "I might take you up on that! Can't get this one to lean back anymore."

After making more inquiries into which of the Camden Superstores the former employee frequented, Dylan said, "I'll call the furniture department there tonight. Go in whenever you're ready and pick out what you want. I'll leave word to have it delivered and set up for you. And anything else you need," he said with a glance around at the retirement apartment that was not shabby but also not luxurious.

Marty arduously got himself back to his feet to walk them to the door, telling them along the way how nice it was to have visitors, how pleased he was to meet them both and thanking Dylan in advance for the new chair he was in line for.

Then Abby and Dylan were outside again, headed for the SUV.

With more knowledge than they'd had before.

And Abby unsure how she should feel about it all.

But grateful that Dylan didn't press her to talk and instead seemed to realize that she needed some space to just process it on her own.

After leaving their visit with Marty Sorensen, Abby and Dylan picked up the lockbox and some fast food for dinner. Then they went back to Abby's apartment.

While they ate burgers and fries at her small kitchen table, they used the key that Gus had sent through the prison chaplain to open the lockbox.

There were no gold coins inside. No key to a safety deposit box full of diamonds. No will making Abby queen of a small country. No obvious treasures at all. Instead there were documents and photographs.

One of the first things Abby took out was Gus Glassman's driver's license.

Marty Sorensen was right, Gus had been a big man with a listed height of six feet five inches and a weight of two hundred and sixty-eight pounds.

Abby studied the picture on the license the way she'd studied the newspaper photo that she'd found on the internet, but again no sense of familiarity came. She did note, though, that he didn't look at all intimidating as he smiled for the camera in that particular picture. Instead, he looked like an amiable enough guy who wouldn't hurt a fly.

She handed the license to Dylan for him to see and took out a birth certificate.

It took a moment before it sank in that it was hers.

"Abby Nicole Glassman," she read out loud. "Huh…" she said, trying the names on to see if they fit.

But she'd always been Abby Crane. Plain Abby Crane. And that's what felt right.

"Does this mean I have to change everything to this name?" she wondered out loud.

"I'm not sure. But I'd say that right now your legal name is Abby Crane, isn't it?"

"That's on the birth certificate I've always used. It was issued when I went into the system."

"So it's valid?"

"It has an embossed stamp—I've been told that's what makes it official."

"Then I'd say that if you wanted to add the Nicole and switch to Glassman you'd probably need to do that through a court."

"But I don't have to."

"I can't see why you would if you don't want to. But I'd think that you should at least have the right date added for your birth."

Abby hadn't thought to look at that part of the certificate and when she did Dylan leaned far enough sideways to see it, too.

"You're eleven days younger than you thought," he said as if that were a positive.

"I suppose I do need to use that," she said, thinking how weird it was to have the birth date she'd always given be different now and repeating it in her head a few times to remember it.

She set her original birth certificate aside and pulled out the rest of the documents in the box.

There was another birth certificate, this one for Anna Lynn Doyle. Born January 3, 1953. And there was also another long-expired driver's license for Anna Lynn Glassman.

"Wow, that could be you," Dylan marveled when they both looked at the picture on that license.

He was right. It was like looking at a photograph of herself and that set off something in her. Some tiny sense of connection.

"That has *got* to be your mother," Dylan added.

Anna Doyle had the same ultra-curly dark hair, the same round, nearly black eyes and the same fair skin. About the only difference was in the way she wore her hair—cut into a short cap the way Abby had been forced to wear hers before she was on her own.

"Strange…" she said softly.

After staring at it for a while Abby set it on top of the pile of other documents on the table.

What came next in the lockbox were pictures galore—none of them in frames, all just loose in the box. And suddenly Abby found herself more curious and inclined to dive into them.

But before she did, Dylan commented that there were dates and notations written on the backs of those that were facedown.

"I'm finished with this burger, how about you?" he asked, glancing at the mostly eaten dinner they'd both been ignoring for some time.

"I've had enough," Abby answered.

"Then how about you let me take these pictures over to your coffee table and organize them chronologically? Then you can look at them in order and get a feel for your timeline."

Abby liked that idea. So while she threw away the burger mess, Dylan took the lockbox and its contents into her tiny living room.

He had all the pictures in one stack for her when she joined him.

The lockbox was on the floor by then, leaving the coffee table free. Abby sat close beside Dylan on the sofa where they both perched forward to look at the photographs together.

Then she took the first one on top of the stack.

"Oh," she breathed the word in pure reflex when what she was seeing hit her.

It was an ordinary photograph of a woman sitting up in a hospital bed, dressed in a hospital gown, holding a swaddled newborn—a mother looking down at the infant she'd just given birth to.

And that infant was Abby.

She'd had a head full of curls right from the start. And rosy-red, full round cheeks. And there was enough of a resemblance even then to stamp her as the child of the woman holding her. A woman smiling, with happy tears glistening in her eyes as she gazed adoringly at her new daughter.

This was not anything Abby had ever imagined or fantasized or dreamed of. It was nothing flashy or glitzy. Yet in its simplicity, in the pure commonplaceness of a mother holding the baby she'd just met, Abby finally began to feel as if this might be real.

Very quietly, as if he knew things were beginning to get to her, Dylan said, "On the back is the name of the hospital where you were born. It's the hospital Gus left you in—maybe he thought by bringing you back there, you'd be safe."

And possibly happy, too, because of the happiness that the young couple had shared there that day, Abby thought when she read the writing on the back. She set the picture on the coffee table and discovered underneath it a second shot much like the first, except that it added the Gus Glassman of the driver's license to the scene. He was also on the hospital bed, his long arms around both mother and child as he beamed down at them.

A lump formed in Abby's throat but she swallowed it.

She and Dylan went through all of the photographs one by one from there, reading what was written on the backs, and laying them out together on the coffee table.

The pictures chronicled the first two years of her life. There were more from the time when her mother must still have been alive, and among those there were many of her with her mother or with her father, either or both of them holding her or looking on.

There did seem to be a gap between when she was about three months old and when she was possibly six or seven months old, and after that it was Abby alone in all the pictures. But it was apparent that she'd been adored, as dozens of tiny events were memorialized, and whenever either or both of her parents were in the shot she could see the love and laughter and pride emanating from them.

"There's a VHS tape in the lockbox," Dylan said when they'd finished with the photographs. "I can take it to our tech guys and have it transferred to—"

"I have a VHS machine," Abby told him. Yes, they were outdated, but on her budget nothing got replaced until it broke. Likely not a concept that a Camden would understand.

Dylan took the tape from the lockbox and handed it to her. "Should I go? Would you rather watch it on your own?" he asked.

"No, it's okay," she said without telling him how much his being there with her through this helped. He was just supportive enough without smothering her. He seemed to know exactly when to give her a moment to herself, a little time and silence to study a photograph. Exactly when to crack a gentle joke or point out to her some telling detail that she was overlooking.

And, for some reason, his perspective, his easy acceptance of what they were seeing as her life, her family, also helped her to begin to accept it as real.

There wasn't much on the videotape. It was a recording of her homecoming from the hospital and then a touching scene of Gus sitting with her in a rocking chair, feeding her a late-night bottle and talking to her about all the things he was going to teach her and how he wouldn't ever let anyone or anything hurt her.

And it was that that brought back the lump in Abby's throat and tears to her eyes to go along with it.

She fought hard to keep from crying. To her, tears

were a sign of weakness that she'd spent a lifetime suppressing.

But there she was, with that videotape playing right in front of her and the man who was her father holding her, feeding her, saying things to her that she'd always longed to hear a father say to her, and nothing she did stopped the tears from rolling down her face.

Dylan didn't say a word. He just put his arms around her, pulled her against his big, hard chest and held her there, a safe haven for a meltdown that came out of pure, raw emotions that suddenly couldn't be contained.

There was no sobbing, only silent tears that coursed down her face while she was cocooned in the warmth of those arms, her head against the rock wall of pectorals that felt strong and powerful enough to protect her from the world.

And no amount of telling herself to stop, to push out of those arms, to reject the solace he was giving her, could make her do it. Instead she stayed where she was, accepting the kind of comfort that was rare to her.

But she wasn't used to being that vulnerable and emotionally exposed, and she fought to stop the tears. Once she'd succeeded, she eased herself away from him.

"I'm sorry. That was dumb," she apologized.

Embarrassed, she stood and went to her bathroom for a tissue that she used to mop herself up in a hurry before coming back to the living room and immediately turning off the television.

"It's me who's sorry," Dylan said, somehow making it easier for her as she rejoined him on the sofa. "Losing your mom was destiny, I guess, but I'm sorry for the part my family had in costing you the dad who obviously loved you a lot."

She almost cried again, but this time years of experience at not showing or giving in to how she felt kicked in to stop it.

"Yeah, I think he did," she said softly, her voice cracking despite her efforts. "And he didn't seem like what I thought he was."

"A bad guy," Dylan filled in.

"How could he be like he was with me and then do what he did for a job?"

"I know it's hard to reconcile. Believe me, I know." He'd already told her that he'd had to learn to separate the men he'd known as loving family from the kind of people they were to outsiders. "But I can't imagine— especially after seeing these pictures and that video— that leaving you didn't just tear that guy apart," he added.

The tears threatened yet again because Abby couldn't imagine that, either. Not now.

"And believe me when I tell you," Dylan added, "that had GiGi known that a two-year-old was being left the way you were—by even just someone who was an employee, let alone that anyone in the family had had anything to do with that child being fatherless—she would never have let it happen."

"So I might have ended up your foster sister?" Abby somehow found the wherewithal to joke.

"Or maybe Margaret and Louie would have ended up with an adopted daughter of their own," he suggested.

"And we would have grown up *like* brother and sister."

He laughed. "Who knows?" he allowed.

Their eyes were locked for a moment and Abby wondered if he was thinking what she was—that she was glad they *hadn't* grown up in any situation that would have resembled a sibling relationship.

But regardless of what he was thinking, out of that momentary silence he drew a deep breath, sighed, and said, "It's getting late and I should let you sleep on all of this."

It was late by then and she had a morning full of errands before the afternoon and evening doing the trial run for his sister's wedding.

And somehow it helped her feel more in control again to be able to deny herself the extra time with him that she still wanted.

So, when he stood to go, she walked him to her door.

"Thanks for all you did—finding Marty Sorensen and taking me to meet him and getting the lockbox." And for tonight when he'd weathered so smoothly her open emotions and brought to it all such a perfect combination of comfort and compassion and humor to help her wade through it.

But that was more than Abby could say.

"It was nothing. I was glad to do it," he said, deflecting her gratitude as he stopped at her apartment door and turned to face her.

He reached a hand to her upper arm and squeezed, sending something warm and glittery all through her. "Are you okay? Will you be okay if I go?"

It almost seemed as if he wanted her to say she wouldn't, that he wanted her to ask him to stay.

And, heaven help her, she wanted to.

But only because of how much she liked being with him. She was accustomed to taking care of herself no matter what the circumstances.

"It's okay," she said. "I'll be fine. I just have to let everything sink in. And remember a new birthday..."

He squeezed her arm again, looking down into her eyes as if searching for a sign that she really would be all right. And that caring, too, was something unfamiliar to her.

Unfamiliar and so sweet and so appealing as well as unusually tempting to her.

Then, when she wasn't thinking at all about anything beyond that, he leaned over and kissed her. Just briefly. Just a brush of his lips to hers.

Yet it was still enough for sparks to erupt in Abby to top off an evening that had already been intensely emotional.

Then it was over, and he straightened up and all she could think was that she wanted him to do it again.

But he didn't. He smiled a small smile that said that kiss might have somehow taken him a little by surprise, too, and said, "If you need anything—*anything*—even just to talk about today, call me. Three in the morning—it doesn't matter."

Abby nodded, thinking that he didn't know that that was not something she would ever do, but appreciating the offer and the fact that he genuinely seemed willing to be her middle-of-the-night sounding board if she needed one.

"I'll see you tomorrow," he said then.

"To be our guard at the gate while we do girlie things," she quipped.

He smiled, and out of the blue he kissed her again—much like the first time, so lightly that his lips were barely touching hers.

Yet it was enough to infuse her with even more confusing feelings when her response was the inclination to fling herself against that big chest of his again and have his arms around her the way they'd been when she was crying.

But she kept a tight hold over those desires and

merely stood there, doing nothing more than tipping her chin up to access and return that simple little kiss before it ended, too.

Dylan said good-night then and she let him out, firmly closing the door behind him before she turned back to that lockbox, those pictures and that videotape.

Only instead of thinking about any of those, it was still Dylan who was on her mind.

Leaving her wondering why, in a long history of keeping all but two people at arm's length, she couldn't seem to keep this guy—of all guys—at least that far away.

Why, even knowing better, it was so impossible for her to want to...

Chapter Six

The trial run for hair, makeup and nails for Lindie Camden's wedding went well on Wednesday.

There was a bit of a glitch when several photographers showed up. They couldn't get into the salon but they knocked on the door and the windows, apparently hoping someone would open up enough for them to snap a candid shot.

Dylan went out the back door and around to the front to deal with them but they wouldn't disband. One of them got angry when Dylan refused to give any information or allow them in and threw a battery pack at him. Dylan ducked to avoid being hit and the pack broke through a pane of the front window.

Dylan handled that by calling the police, who rounded up the paparazzi and took them in on trespassing and vandalism charges.

Luckily no other newshounds replaced them and one phone call from Dylan brought someone to replace the pane of glass while he rigged a partition to continue to protect his family's privacy.

In the meantime, the Camden wedding party kept Abby and the two other hairstylists on her team, plus China, the other makeup artists and both manicurists busy well into Wednesday evening.

GiGi and Margaret—neither of whom had been scheduled—had been persuaded to come along at the last minute so there were two more than expected. But surprises like that didn't ruffle Abby's team and they made the best of it.

Because of the additions, though, the session went on longer than expected, and by the time everyone had had their turn, it was past eight o'clock.

Dylan also took it upon himself to call for a stretch limousine and two security personnel to pick up the by-then somewhat inebriated women and he confiscated the keys of those who had driven. He assured them that he would have their cars in their driveways by morning, then he sent them off to an impromptu dinner in a private room of one of Denver's finest restaurants, with the two security guards going along just in case any photographers got wind of the unplanned meal.

Abby had kept her team longer than planned and so sent them all on their way, too, staying herself to clean up while Dylan called in more security people to get the abandoned cars home. It was nearly ten o'clock when everything was accomplished and the two of them could call it a day.

"Food!" Dylan said in a cry of desperation at that point.

"There's a box of emergency cookies," Abby informed him as she put away the shop's vacuum cleaner.

"I need more than that and you must, too. I munched

on the same stuff the girls did but I never saw you eat a thing."

And she knew he'd done more than his fair share of watching her because she'd caught him at it and felt his eyes on her most of the time she'd been working.

"How's that place across the street and how do you feel about seafood?" he asked then.

"I like their fish and chips," she answered, knowing full well that she should beg off, send him on his way—and certainly not accept even a casual invitation to a late-night meal with him.

But out had come the encouraging words anyway, because she just couldn't seem to say no when it came to this guy.

"Oh, yeah! Salty, vinegary fish, ketchup on the fries—yes, yes, yes!"

Abby laughed at his rapture. "You *are* hungry, aren't you?"

"Starving! Are we done here?"

"Are all the cars but yours and mine gone?" she asked, just to torture him by prolonging this.

"Gone!" he proclaimed.

Abby pointed her chin in the direction of the window that had been replaced in such a hurry. "All safe and secure?"

"A hundred percent," he clipped out like a rookie answering his superior's demand.

She looked around the salon that she'd put back in order. "Am I done?"

"Spotless! Now let's go eat!"

She laughed at him again. "I'll get my purse and check the back door," she said, leaving him in the salon while she went to do that.

Alone in the supply room where she'd left her purse,

she did a quick check in a mirror on the wall as she removed the smock that covered her jeans and her double layer of T-shirts—a navy blue V-neck over a pale blue tank top.

She'd left her own hair loose again today, so she scrunched it to freshen it a bit and was glad that she hadn't applied her makeup until just before coming here this afternoon because it still looked okay.

She reapplied her lip gloss, tugged at the hem of her T-shirt to make sure it was in the right place—adjusting her posture at the same time—then went back to Dylan.

He was wearing charcoal slacks and a white dress shirt with the sleeves rolled to his elbows—nothing special and yet to her he looked fantastic. As usual.

Especially because, as time had passed, he'd developed that bit of dark scruff that gave him the bad-boy edge she liked so much.

She flipped the switch that turned off the lights in the rear portion of the salon and joined him at the front door, which she locked behind them as they exited.

Taking in a deep breath of the cooler night air, he stretched his neck and pulled his broad shoulders so far back she heard something in him crack.

"That was a lot of hours of sitting through hair and makeup," he groaned as she turned around just in time to enjoy the spectacle.

The restaurant was nearly empty at that hour, so they were seated immediately. Dylan didn't wait to be asked, ordering food and drinks from the girl who luckily happened to be the waitress as well as the hostess, since staff was at a minimum by then, too. He also charmed her into bringing drinks and shrimp cocktails in a hurry.

Then he stretched again and Abby reveled in watching from across the table, her gaze riding along on those mile-wide shoulders before he seemed to truly relax and settle in.

He took a swig of the beer he'd ordered and said, "You and your team are stars. Thirteen women and every one of them went away happy—that's an accomplishment."

"They were all pretty easy to please." Abby deflected the praise.

"No they weren't," he countered with a laugh. "And when GiGi sat down for China to do her makeup—" Another laugh. "I was waiting to see if my grandmother would come away with all that dark eye stuff China wears herself and the holy-cow lipstick. And about that same time you talked Margaret into a haircut—hair that Margaret has worn the same way for my entire life— and I thought *oh, boy, here we go, this is gonna be a disaster…*"

Abby just smiled.

"Instead the two of them ended up thrilled—like little girls somebody had just turned into princesses. Wow, you're good! You and China."

"We try." More humility because, while Abby was proud of what she could accomplish, she wasn't comfortable with too much praise. A simple "thanks" was enough.

Their meals came while they were still munching on the shrimp cocktails and as they began eating fish and chips, as well, Dylan said, "Come to work for us."

Abby laughed. "I *am* working for you—I worked for you today, and since everybody was happy with what we did, we'll be working for you through the wedding."

Dylan shook his head. "After that. This whole wedding-hair thing has made us all realize that the salons in our stores—and the people working them—aren't up to Camden standards anymore."

Up to Camden standards...

That phrase triggered wariness in Abby. It was so close to what Mark had said over and over to her—that he was just trying to bring her *up to par.* It made her feel bad for the people Dylan was referring to who weren't up to Camden *standards*—which were no doubt higher than Mark's.

But while she might feel bad for whoever Dylan was talking about, she was grateful it *wasn't* her who was falling short. This time, at least.

"We know now that we need a major overhaul," he was saying when she refocused. "The salons themselves have to be updated and made more appealing—especially to younger clients. And the staff needs to be weeded through. We have to hire new people who work at your caliber and let go of the ones doing a bad job. So come to work for us, revamp us from top to bottom, then we could have you oversee and run the entire salon department for all our stores nationwide."

Oh. She hadn't been expecting *that!*

It took her off guard and before she'd thought about the inappropriateness of the response, she said, "Yuck."

"Yuck?" he parroted with a quizzical chuckle. "I make you a legitimate job offer and you say yuck?"

That would have been Mark's sentiment.

"Sorry," Abby apologized out of long habit before she said, "That just sounds so...*business-y*..."

He laughed a little more genuinely. *"Business-y?* Well, yeah, a job offer is business. But what is it you do if it isn't a business?"

"I do hair."

"But you manage the salon you work at, right? That

has to mean doing the same work that I want you to do for us."

"I don't fire people, that's up to Sheila—the woman who owns the shops. I tell her when I think someone isn't working out but she does the actual letting-go herself so she can make sure no one comes back and sues her."

"Sure. You'd only be making the decision for us, too. We have a process and people for that for the same reason, so it wouldn't be you personally giving anybody the boot. But you've had experience spotting who isn't working out and who needs to go—"

"My least favorite part of the job."

"I saw you today, though, and you handle everybody who works with you well. And China told me that it was you who lobbied for expansion of the shop you're in now when the storefront next door closed. It was you who came up with the whole remodel idea that went so well your boss had you do it for her other shop."

"Maybe China should switch to public relations," Abby muttered as she ate, feeling uncomfortable with his push for this.

"We'll get our design people in to meet with you, hear your ideas, then they'll present what they come up with. You can pick and choose what works and what doesn't. You're a great stylist and you put the Beauty By Design special events team together—every one of them almost as good as you are. That means you can spot talent, right?"

A shrug was her only answer.

"Just come and do all that for us. Then you can launch Camden's own special occasions teams for every store, too, and work with Vonni."

Vonni was engaged to his older brother Dane. She'd

been a private wedding consultant until meeting Dane, and now worked with Camden Superstores. She was also part of Lindie's wedding party and Abby had met her at the Camden's Sunday dinner and done her hair today. She liked her. But that still didn't make anything he was saying more interesting to her.

"I like my job the way it is," she told him. "I like doing hair, I like getting to know my regulars, keeping up with them and their families. They get to be like friends—last time I was sick, one of my older clients brought me chicken soup. I wouldn't be able to have relationships like that with what you're talking about. I'd be a manager, not a stylist. And I told you what I like about doing special events and getting to be a part of so many of those occasions for people. I don't want to go from that to being some kind of—"

"Executive? Because that's what I'll make you," he went on enthusiastically. "An executive with your own assistant and your own secretary. You'd have an executive's salary and benefits. You'd have an office downtown in our building. You'd travel for us and see the country, even Europe if you want. There'd be a car, and paid vacation time, and perks that I know you don't have doing what you're doing. You told me you've changed jobs a lot so I know you can't be afraid to do that. Only every change has been a lateral move. This time you can take one, big giant leap up the ladder."

Abby stared at him, aware that she was wide-eyed. "How come every time I'm with you, you knock me for a loop with something else?" she asked, sounding as dazed as she again felt over something he was presenting to her.

"It's not my goal," he said. "I just sat there today

watching you and thinking about this stuff, and thinking that you're wasted on such a small scale."

She took a drink of her iced tea and then a bite of fish to buy herself time, knowing that when something like this was offered to her, she should at least think about it—that that was what China would tell her.

So she thought about it.

But she didn't have to think about it for long because the whole thing just felt wrong.

She shook her head once more and said, "I graduated high school and went to cosmetology school—a *trade* school. What you're talking about is a job for somebody who went to college. Who went to graduate school. That isn't me. I'm happy being just a stylist and running my little shop."

"That somebody else owns."

"What you're talking about is just more than I can handle."

"Don't underestimate yourself, Abby."

"I don't think I am. I'm just thinking about where I'm happy and what I'm happy doing."

"But you could do so much more. I'll be your education. I'll teach you whatever you need to know—"

"I just wouldn't fit in to what you're talking about."

"Sure you would. Or could, eventually. I'll walk you through everything—whether it's the job itself or maneuvering the corporate world or business dinners and parties, or dressing for the job—"

"I'm doing just fine the way I am," she insisted, hearing defensiveness creeping into her own tone and feeling it rising in her, too.

"But you could do so much better if you'd just let me help—"

"I know what *help* means. It means fixing me. And I don't need fixing," she said firmly.

"Of course you don't need fixing," he said, sounding confused. "I'm just saying that no matter what kind of education or experience you've had—"

"You're saying we can keep it under wraps, right? We can just not tell anyone where I came from or that I was a *foster kid*—because that can be off-putting and make people think that I was messed up. Or at least that I've had ties to other bad, messed up kids so I could have picked up all kinds of *unpalatable* tricks and traits. We can keep where I came from and how much education I *don't* have our little secret," she said, repeating not only things Mark had said, but stereotypes she'd encountered along the way.

"I can be your very own pet improvement project," she accused heatedly. "You can change me, mold me. You can teach me how to dress better and how to not wear tacky jewelry—" She flippantly flicked the hoop in her left ear. "If I'd just cut my hair or at least make sure to tie it back so it isn't so *wild,* and if I make sure to stay right by you at those business dinners and parties and not say too much—because, after all, it wouldn't be any fun for me to have to keep up with conversations that I wouldn't understand anyway. Instead I can just listen and learn. Maybe you'll even come up with a backstory for me that I can tell to cover up—"

"Whoa!" Dylan said, his voice just loud enough to override hers. "Is *that* what it seemed like I was saying to you?"

To her it was. To her, that was where he was headed and the real intent behind his words.

"Like I said, I know what *help* means," she informed him, reining in her temper to speak more calmly. "I learned it from the last man who wanted to *help* me *be a better Abby*—that's what he called it. What it really meant was that he was ashamed me, of what I do, of who I am, of where I came from. At the end, when he wasn't interested in being diplomatic because I was ending things with him, he said he'd been trying to do me a favor by polishing a—"

"If you're going to say what I think you're going to say, don't."

Because he probably thought she was crass. Mark had. Although those particularly crude and hurtful words had been Mark's.

Rather than saying them Abby amended the phrasing. "He was trying to put a shine on me because he was embarrassed by my background, my lack of higher education and what he called my *unsophisticated* nature. Or, at least, that's what he called it when he was trying to be nice. At the end he just said that I was *from the streets*. A low class piece of trash that my own parents hadn't wanted. And he guessed he was wrong to think he could fix that."

For a moment Abby thought she saw Dylan's temper rise. His jaw was tight and a muscle on one side of it visibly flexed.

He must be mad at her for speaking to him the way she had, especially in answer to a job offer. She was aware that she'd probably overreacted, but this was still a sensitive subject for her.

"I don't know who that guy is but somebody should set him very, very straight," he said.

He was mad at *Mark*?

China had been when she'd told her friend the things Mark had said. But China came from the same background—she'd been just as personally insulted by

Mark's idea that all foster kids were trash as Abby was. Why did Dylan care?

Then he shook his head and clearly put some effort into relaxing and refocusing his attention solely on her. In a softer, kinder, much more sympathetic voice that invited her confidence, he said, "Who was this guy?"

For some reason, Dylan getting his back up at Mark made her less defensive all of a sudden.

"His name was Mark Peterson—my only attempt at a long-term relationship," she admitted.

"You've only had one?"

Another shrug. "I've been told that I keep people—especially men—at a distance." Something she wished she could do more of with *this* man and didn't understand why she couldn't. "After Mark," she said fatalistically, "maybe that's for the best."

"How long were you with him?"

She'd already revealed so much it seemed silly to conceal anything else. "Mark and I dated for a year, then we lived together for another year—for some of that time, we were engaged. I don't know why he wanted to marry me, but he proposed and I'd…" She shrugged one more time. "I'd let myself get in deep enough to think it might work out."

"Sure," Dylan said as if he didn't know why she wouldn't have. "But then he started doing all that stuff—with the clothes and the jewelry and the keeping quiet at parties and a *backstory*?"

Abby took a deep breath and pushed away what remained of her food, no longer having an appetite.

"It wasn't only after we were engaged. It was all along. But he was subtle about it at first, and like I said, it was always supposed to be for my own good. To make me a *better Abby*," she repeated the phrase Mark had so sweetly said to her...until the break-up, when he'd lashed out at her with his genuine opinion. "What it took me some time to realize—and that *didn't* happen until after we were engaged—was that it really boiled down to him thinking I wasn't good enough for him—"

"And he was what? King of the World?"

Abby took that comment with a grain of salt, unable to forget the exchange she'd overheard with Cade at the Camden Sunday dinner.

Besides, there had been people all through her life who had had similar preconceived notions of who or what she was because of the way she'd grown up. Mark wasn't the first.

"Mark is a systems analyst from a normal, middle-class family in the suburbs," she said without editorializing.

"Who looks down pretty severely on kids in and from foster care."

"Yes. But he isn't alone in that—I've met a lot of people who don't have the best opinion of foster care kids. People who didn't want their kids to play with the foster kid in their class. People who didn't trust a foster kid to babysit for them. People all along who were leery of me because of where I came from and who were afraid I was defective in some way—"

"Defective?" he repeated, as if it was a dirty word.

Abby didn't know what to do but shrug again. "That's been said," she confirmed before she went on. "And when I figured out that Mark shared those ideas and that he thought I wasn't good enough for him or his family, I broke up with him." And discovered herself even more wary of relationships.

But she didn't say that.

"Why was he with you in the first place if he thought that?"

"He didn't know about my background at first. It isn't my opening line on a date. I think he liked me, and then he found out so he tried to make things line up for himself."

"How long has it been over?" Dylan asked as if he didn't want to comment on her assumption.

"About a year."

"It had to have hurt," he said softly.

"Sure," she said, though she tried to make it sound as if she'd taken it in stride. She didn't want to show weakness by admitting it had pulled the rug out from under her and left her hiding out at China's apartment, barely able to do her job and slink back there every day until she could get a place of her own.

"But maybe I'm just better off on my own like I've always been," she added. "Better off taking care of myself, looking out for myself." Even though, deep down, she kind of wanted that not to be true.

Dylan didn't say anything but she thought she read skepticism in the expression on that refined face as he pushed away what remained of his own meal.

Then he looked at her squarely, earnestly, and said, "I didn't mean to imply I thought there was anything wrong with you with what I said about the job. I just know that it would be a pretty monumental change for you to go from what you're doing to what I'd like you to do for us. To keep you from being overwhelmed, I'd walk you through it the whole way until you got used to it and knew all the ins and outs." Then he smiled that smile that had just a hint of wickedness to it, glanced at the mass of curls around her face and said, "And I'm the last guy who would want to see that untamed hair tamed—I think it's great."

Okay, he recouped some points with that because it was an issue with such history for her.

"I am serious, though," he persisted. "I can see you accomplishing much bigger things. Making more money. Becoming more successful. I don't think you recognize just how smart and talented you are. I think China knows it about you, but—"

"China thinks bigger than I do but she isn't always right."

"She's more out there, more flamboyant, maybe. But I think she knows you and she seems to see the same things in you that I do. So you might consider that she's right to think that you could do bigger things."

"I don't want your job," Abby said concisely. "I like what I do."

"You do it well," he said, as if that wrapped up a conversation that had gotten away from him and gone places he'd never expected. Then, more under his breath, he added, "And the systems analyst wasn't good enough for you."

It was a nice thing to say even if Abby didn't take it to heart.

The restaurant was closing, and since they were finished Dylan paid the bill and they went outside again. Retracing their steps across the street, they walked around to the dimly lit parking lot behind the shop.

Along the way he said, "So, tomorrow I'm sneaking Lindie into the regular shop for what?"

"Highlights that we didn't have time for today."

"And you have a back door in and a private room there where you can do it?"

"Sort of. When Sheila first started, the salon was her

husband's barber shop. He let her have a station of her own in back and built a wall so her customers and his were separated. When Sheila's business started doing better than her husband's he turned over the whole place to her and went to work for someone else. She expanded into the front but she didn't bother to take down the wall—"

"Yeah, now that I think about it, I do remember a wall in back."

"We don't actually use that station too much," Abby went on. "Only in a pinch if we're really busy. But, yeah, if you and Lindie come in through the break-room door and go from there to that old station, nobody will even know you guys are there. But you'll have to get there without photographers or anybody following you because the rest of the shop will be open for business. Anyone could come in the front and charge through till they find you."

"I'll make sure we don't have a tail."

They'd reached the parking lot by then. Abby's compact car was near the building. Parked on the side street just outside of the lot was a sleek black Jaguar but the SUV she'd ridden in with him twice now wasn't anywhere in sight.

"Where's your car?" she asked.

"That one is mine," he said with a nod to the sports car as he walked by it to go with her to hers. "I use the SUV when I know I'll have more than one passenger, but this is my baby. I just got her back from the body shop today."

"Were you in a wreck?"

They'd reached the driver's door of her car and he'd pivoted around to face her so she saw his grimace in the lot's single light.

"No, luckily not a wreck. But the damage *was* done by someone else…"

He didn't elaborate so Abby unlocked her door and opened it, standing with it between them.

"What would you say to coming with me to the rehearsal dinner on Friday night?" he asked out of the blue.

"Are you asking just because I told you I like to get a peek at the festivities? Or because I'll already be at GiGi's house to do hair before—"

"This is not some kind of pity invite," he swore. "Well, unless you want to think of it as taking pity on me and being my only ally again—Sunday Dinner, The Sequel. I was just thinking that I'd like it if you were there with me. As my plus one. Just because… I want you there."

"I don't know that you're winning points with your family by hanging out with the help," she said, recalling once more what she'd overheard at Sunday dinner.

"Don't kid yourself—at this point, they like you better than they like me."

She doubted that.

But she did want to go. She tried to deny it, but she couldn't. She liked the Camdens. And even if it was only a temporary, for-now association with her as a service provider, they were all warm and friendly toward her; they didn't make her feel like The Help butting in on private family occasions. And it was a chance for her to actually *be* at one of those special events she usually only got to view from the sidelines.

And even if all of that hadn't been true, there was also the fact—and the real reason she couldn't deny herself—that it was a chance to be with Dylan.

"Come on," he urged. "Everybody is meeting at GiGi's to go over to the church so you'll be right there.

If you want to change clothes GiGi has plenty of rooms you can use. And, who knows, maybe it would be good for you to see the setting of the whole thing beforehand. Maybe you'll say, *oh, your hair has to be higher than we were planning, Lindie, to compete with those cathedral ceilings.*"

Abby laughed. "I don't think I'm going to make anybody's hair high enough to compete with cathedral ceilings."

She knew he was only joking, but his grin would have given it away if she hadn't. The grin that crinkled his gorgeous blue eyes and drew lines to accentuate that mouth that had kissed her the night before…

"Just say yes," he commanded.

What was there about this guy that got to her so much?

"Yes…" she said, even though she knew she should say no and didn't understand why she couldn't. "If you're sure your family—"

"I'm sure."

The grin had mellowed into a small smile as he seemed to study her face as if it was important to him to know every inch of it.

Then he leaned over the top of the door and found her mouth with his again in a kiss that began like the two simple little kisses of the night before and then went further.

His lips parted over hers and it became a very real kiss. Not a comforting kiss. Not a quickie kiss. But a kiss kiss.

Especially when his hand came to the back of her head, when his fingers threaded through her hair to hold her more firmly to that mouth that was moving over hers and lingering long enough for her to kiss him in return. For her to taste the mints they'd both popped after dinner, for her to feel the warmth and strong softness of his lips and judge him the best kisser she'd ever encountered.

That scruff of beard wasn't as rough against her face as she'd expected it to be and she liked that, too. That bit of masculine coarseness against the smoothness of her skin.

The way he lingered let her know he didn't hate it, either. Then he ended it, without any eagerness, and peered down into her eyes.

"I'm pretty sure that I like you too much, Abby Crane," he whispered, maybe more to himself than to her.

Then he kissed her again, just as potently but only for a moment before he stepped back.

"I'll see you tomorrow for highlights," he said then.

She laughed. "You want some, too?"

"No, thanks, I think I'll pass," he answered with another grin, this one slightly crooked.

Then he kissed her a third time, quickly, there and gone, as if he just couldn't not do it, before he stepped away completely.

Abby took it as a signal to get behind the wheel of her car and when she did he closed her door and said through the window, "Lock it and drive safe."

She did lock the door before she started the engine and he got out of the way so she could head for the parking lot's exit.

She watched him through her rearview mirror as he got into the sports car and disappeared from her sight.

But what didn't disappear was the memory of his hand in her hair. Of his mouth on hers.

Of those kisses she only wanted more of right at that minute.

Those kisses that could carry her away somewhere she knew better than to go...

Chapter Seven

"I don't know why you're here this morning, but, man, is it nice to see a familiar face that isn't peeved at me!" Dylan greeted his cousin Seth.

Seth lived in Northbridge, Montana, running the farm there and the rest of Camden Incorporated's nationwide agricultural affairs. He and his wife, Lacey, had come in to Denver with their new baby for Lindie's wedding. They were staying with GiGi, so Seth showing up at Dylan's loft early Thursday morning was a surprise.

"I brought doughnuts," Seth announced, holding up a bag as he did.

"I've got coffee," Dylan contributed, leading the way into his kitchen.

Seth perched on a bar stool on one side of the island counter while Dylan went to the other side of it to pour two mugs of steaming dark French roast.

"Everybody's giving you a hard time, huh?" Seth said as they each chose a doughnut.

"Not without cause. But oh, yeah!" Dylan answered emphatically.

Because Seth and his wife didn't live in Denver they had only met Lara once and not for long enough to have been drawn into her antics. So Seth and his wife were the sole members of the family who weren't unhappy with him.

"I had to get out of here until Lara moved on to greener pastures—that's why I went to Europe. But I think those three months away just made everything with the family fester. Since I've been back..." Dylan shook his head and exhaled a frustrated sigh. "Let's just say there's been lots of fallout from the Lara debacle."

"I think everybody's coming around, though."

"Are they?" Dylan asked hopefully, knowing that Seth had likely heard much that wouldn't be said directly to Dylan.

"They all know you're working hard to make it up to them and they appreciate the effort you're going to. It's just that—"

"The way they see it, I turned on them."

"Well, you definitely didn't take their side. And that raised some hackles. But it'll pass. It's already in the process of passing. What do you think they're gonna do, kick you out of the family?"

"Some days since I've been back it's seemed like that might be a possibility."

"Nah! Mostly the talk I've heard since I got in yesterday morning has been about this hairdresser girl you're working on to make amends. Everyone's focused on wondering about you and her."

"Me and her? There's no me and her. But they like her, right?"

"They all seem to like her a lot, yeah."

Dylan laughed as he finished a bite of doughnut and washed it down with a drink of coffee. "They're probably worried about her being anywhere near me," he said facetiously.

"Nah," Seth answered as if that was silly. "But I think they might be worried that something is up between the two of you and that it's too soon after Lara, that your head might not be straight yet. That whole thing was pretty messed up."

"I'm completely over Lara, no matter what they might think," Dylan said, having no doubt about that himself. "So my head is straight enough to know that I have to heal wounds with the family before I move on to anything else. Like a new relationship."

"Sounds like you're pretty clear about that," Seth observed. "But everybody's saying that whenever this Abby girl is around you turn to...you know...mush."

"I'm just being nice to her," Dylan protested, in spite of knowing that he *felt* as if he turned to mush whenever he was with Abby—and even when he wasn't. Like whenever he just thought about her, which was pretty much every minute. But he didn't know it showed and he certainly wasn't going to admit to it.

Seth drank coffee and shrugged before he said, "Lacey noticed it yesterday. She said in a room full of women—some of them Lindie's hot friends and some of them hot girls working on everybody—you barely took your eyes off of this Abby."

"Now I'm in trouble for *not* ogling Lindie's friends and the women who were doing the work?"

Seth laughed. "Sometimes we can't win, can we?" he commiserated. "But just between you and me...*is* something going on with this new girl?"

Was something going on with Abby?

There was the constant thinking about her.

And picturing her in his mind.

And falling asleep every night craving things he shouldn't be craving with her.

There was the ever-present struggle to keep his hands to himself whenever he was with her, when he wanted to reach out and stroke her face or test a strand of that untamed hair or touch her arm or hold her hand or anything that would make contact.

And there was the kissing…

"Nah," Dylan said, echoing his cousin. "I mean, I like her. She's great. But like I said, I know the dust has to settle—for me and for the family—before I get into anything else."

Seth nodded but his expression seemed to convey skepticism. "I'm sure you're being careful," he said.

Dylan thought that was more advice than confidence, but he only said, "I am," reminding himself of the necessity to be cautious even as he reassured his cousin.

But it was a reminder he knew he needed one way or another.

Because when he was with Abby, lines seemed to blur that shouldn't.

After Lara he couldn't help being leery of the fact that what he saw in someone was possibly not all there was to them. That there could be plenty of underlying issues that he should be on the lookout for. Issues that could have dire consequences.

And last night Abby had shown him something of herself that had taken him by surprise. Which could be an indication of that, he thought.

He'd been aware even before last night that she kept her cards close to the vest, that she was extremely self-protective, and that she wasn't the most trusting person he'd ever encountered.

Given how she'd grown up, that was understandable.

And what went along with it all was that she was also strong and fiercely independent, that she wasn't needy or grasping, that she was determined to take care of herself.

Coming post-Lara, all of that was particularly appealing to him. Yet, while focusing on that, he hadn't bothered to think about what other underlying issues there could be.

But last night she'd flared over his job offer, of all things, and that had surprised him.

She'd misinterpreted what he'd been saying to her. Nowhere in any of what he'd suggested had he intended to criticize her or say that she was lacking or needed fixing or improving, and he honestly didn't see how she'd taken that from it. But she had.

And she'd gotten really defensive about it. She'd dismissed what he had honestly been proposing and focused solely on the impression she'd had that she was somehow not good enough. Her back had definitely been up. Over something he'd thought was a pretty sweet job offer. Something anyone else would have jumped at. Or at least been flattered by. Yet it had served only to provoke her.

And while she'd explained her reaction and he'd come to understand that it had roots in a relationship that had hurt her, it had also seemed like a curtain opening to show him that other side of her. A side that included some of those underlying issues he'd learned not to ignore.

Granted, what he'd faced in Abby had been a woman who was hot under the collar over something that turned out to be a sensitive issue rather than a woman who was making claims against his family and pounding wedges between them all. But it was that difference between what he thought, what he assumed, what he expected and what she'd come at him with that had given him pause.

So, yes, he needed to be careful. Especially when he was so taken with her. When he was increasingly susceptible to her. Especially when every minute with her—other than that response to his job offer—made him like her even more.

"I'm not going to let anything go too far with Abby," he said to his cousin then. "I've shaken up her whole world with what we've uncovered about her history— she has a lot to come to terms with. And, God knows, I have my own problems at the moment."

Seth frowned at him. "You're not going to let anything get too far with her? Does that mean that there *is* something going on?"

"Just that I like her is all." Dylan conceded only to what he'd already admitted. "Another time, another place, different circumstances, would I maybe explore it a little? Yeah, maybe. But not here and now. I'm just doing what GiGi has asked me to do and I'm grateful that it isn't painful."

And he was determined to put the brakes on things like kissing Abby because he knew he shouldn't have done that.

Any more than he should be wanting so damn much to do it again.

But he was going to resist. He was.

"So you're doing chauffeur duty today?" Seth asked as he finished his coffee.

Dylan was relieved to let the subject change naturally. "I'm at Lindie's disposal, yeah," he said. "The final dress fitting and something about picking up gifts for her attendants, and then I'm taking her to Abby's salon for highlights in her hair."

Seth grimaced. "Wow, you *are* paying your dues."

Actually, while he wasn't looking forward to any of what he was doing with his sister, he *did* consider seeing Abby at the end of the day his reward for it all.

He didn't say that, though.

Instead he said, "Lindie would probably need me to do it for security purposes, anyway. Every day closer to the wedding makes the group of photographers and newshounds grow. I'm even using a rental car today so we won't be driving around in anything that might give us away—actually, it's a van that looks like a delivery van. I have it arranged so another security person picks her up at home and takes her to the Colorado Boulevard store as if she's doing last minute wedding stuff there. Then I'll be waiting for her at the delivery dock to get her out incognito so—hopefully—we won't be followed."

Seth nodded. "Want help? I'm probably the least recognizable Camden since I don't live around here, so I could tag along and keep you company while Lindie does the fluff stuff."

Dylan would have liked to have the cousin he didn't get to see enough of tag along today.

Until it came time for that reward at the end of it all.

Then having Seth with him would just seem like a distraction from Abby. A buffer that he didn't want.

It was exactly what he should have agreed to for exactly that reason.

But he couldn't make himself do it.

"Thanks, but I think the fewer of us there are, the better."

"Then I should probably let you get going. I just wanted to say hey and see how you were holding up."

"I'm okay," Dylan assured his cousin as he walked him to the elevator.

But just how okay was he if his biggest goal today—despite everything—was to get any time he could with Abby?

"That needs to sit for about twenty minutes. Can I get you guys coffee or tea or a soda?" Abby asked Lindie and Dylan when she'd finished wrapping the bride-to-be's hair in strips of foil.

"I'd love an iced tea," Lindie said.

"Nothing for me," Dylan answered from where he was sitting on a folding chair that Abby had pulled into the more secluded portion of the salon for him.

And positioned in the corner that she could see from the mirror as she worked.

It was stupid, she told herself.

But it made her own time pass so much more pleasantly to be able to steal glimpses of him whenever she wanted—which was about every thirty seconds. Glimpses of him sitting there with his arms crossed over his chest, massive biceps stretching the short sleeves of his polo shirt, the ankle of one long leg propped on the thick, muscular thigh of the other, and looking altogether masculine and sooo hunky...

"I'll be right back," she said to Lindie, leaving the two of them to go out into the front portion of the salon.

"Ah, there she is. This is Abby Crane—she's who you want to talk to about wedding hair."

One of the other stylists in the salon was at the desk and seemed relieved to pass off the attractive blonde woman whom Abby had assumed was a customer coming or going.

Abby had no choice but to make a detour from where she'd been headed.

"Hi," she greeted the blonde, who wore her hair in a chin-length, very precisely cut bob, and whose eye makeup China would say was the wrong color for her hazel eyes.

"I'm Lara Humphrey."

She said that as if her name should be recognizable, but Abby had no idea who she was.

"I want to talk to you about possibly doing hair and makeup for my wedding."

"Sure," Abby said.

She caught China as China passed through the salon and asked if she would take an iced tea to the back station.

About that time the other stylist removed herself from behind the desk and turned her back to the blonde so she could roll her eyes at Abby to warn her that the blonde was a handful.

Abby took the stylist's place behind the desk.

"Congratulations on your engagement," Abby began. "When is your wedding?"

"I'm not sure of the exact date yet—it will definitely be in December but we haven't decided between the two days that the country club is making available to us."

"Okay," Abby said. "So you have a little bit of time. You might want to make an appointment with me or one of the other people on the special events team to just have us do your next haircut or style—something that can give you an idea of what we can do. Then, if you like that, we can go from there. That's less costly than scheduling a test run for your whole wedding party at this point—"

"Cost isn't an issue," the woman clipped out. "I've heard that you're doing Lindie Camden's wedding."

There was nothing to indicate that this woman might be a photographer or a reporter who had tracked Lindie and Dylan to the salon. She was dressed in very expensive slacks and a cashmere sweater set with pearls that looked real. Abby might not shop for designer labels herself, but she had worked with enough wealthy clients to recognize pricey, high-quality clothes—certainly not anything that the kind of reporter who stalked celebrities would be able to afford. And she was wearing what Abby guessed to be about a three-carat diamond engagement ring on her finger. Plus she only had a small purse on a chain over her shoulder that wasn't large enough to conceal anything other than credit cards and a cell phone.

Since there weren't any other newspeople gathered outside—the way there had been at the special occasions salon on Wednesday—it didn't seem that word had leaked that Lindie and Dylan were there. There was also the woman's demanding, entitled attitude that spoke of something else.

But before Abby could answer her question about whether or not she was doing the Camden wedding, the blonde said, "If you're doing that one, I want you to do mine."

That sounded purely competitive and added to Abby's thought that this was not a photographer or a reporter. So she continued to treat her as a potential customer.

"We recommend that you try out the kind of work we do, see our price list and what services we offer. If you come in for a solo appointment, we can talk about—"

"*Are* you doing the Camden wedding?" the blonde demanded.

Her voice had suddenly raised to interrupt Abby and carried far enough through the shop for stylists and customers to be glancing toward the desk. Abby had no idea if it was carrying all the way to the back station where Lindie and Dylan would be able to hear.

"We don't talk about what events we are or aren't doing," Abby said so noncommittally that she could have easily been trying not to reveal that they *didn't* have the Camdens' business in order to attract someone who wanted the salon that did.

Which might have been the way the blonde took it, because she said, "You should be glad if you aren't working with those people. They're horrible human beings."

The woman craned to look around Abby, her gaze going from one chair to the next to check out who was sitting in each of them.

Maybe she was a reporter, after all.

But still, that wasn't the sense Abby was getting.

"How many people would there be in your party?" she asked, to steer the conversation in a different direction.

But the blonde was intractable. "I know you're doing that wedding," she said accusingly. "The Camdens and I have friends in common who know it and told me. Friends who knew I was actually engaged to one of them. Until I found out he didn't have a spine and then I called it off."

"And now you've found Mr. Right," Abby said cheerfully, dismissing the rest.

"I have. I dodged *that* bullet, that's for sure. And believe me, it was a big bullet to dodge. I've never met people more hurtful and backstabbing and underhanded!

They deserve all the bad things that get said about them, and then some."

"That's funny because I've heard that they're very nice people."

"Well, someone is lying to you!"

"So what would you like to schedule?" Abby asked, again attempting to do what this woman had claimed she was there for.

"What are you doing for *them*? I want at least what they're getting."

"I meant would you like to schedule a single appointment to get a feel for our work or a special occasions package for you and your wedding party?"

"One of my bridal showers is in two weeks," she announced imperiously and still not quietly. "I guess I could come in just before that. You *must* be good if the almighty Camdens are using you instead of their own precious salons. The *clan* doesn't very often go beyond their own *empire* to do anything. That's the problem—they're all about themselves and their little clique. They're *horrible* to anyone who doesn't turn their back on everything *but* them. It's like they're a cult or something."

Abby had had about enough of that. "You know," she said, acting as if she were pulling up the schedule on the computer screen that the woman couldn't see. "I'd better check December before we go any further…" She paused then shook her head. "Oh, I'm sorry. We're already booked solid that whole month. Unless your date changes—"

"It won't," the blonde said bitingly.

"Then I just can't help you."

The blonde apparently didn't like not getting her way because she threw a bit of a snit that Abby took with a blank expression and without comment, waiting for it to pass.

Then the woman finally turned and left, and as Abby watched her go she couldn't help wondering which of the Camdens could possibly have been dumb enough to be involved with her.

"It was you she was engaged to?" Abby exclaimed.

The shop had closed by the time she'd finished Lindie's hair. Lindie's fiancé, Sawyer, had picked her up, and Dylan had persuaded Abby to have dinner with him.

She knew she should have begged off. But besides wanting to have dinner with him—which she couldn't deny that she did—the visit from Lara Humphrey had left her curious.

When she'd returned to the back station, to Lindie and Dylan, after the blonde had left, neither of them had said anything to lead her to think they'd overheard the woman's rant.

But they'd both been very, very quiet. A whole lot quieter than they'd been before that. They'd even seemed more reserved with each other, and Abby had sensed tension that hadn't been in the air before.

She had to believe that they'd heard. The woman certainly hadn't made any effort to keep her voice down.

And she wondered if Dylan might bring it up over dinner.

So she'd gone along with his idea to drive their respective vehicles to her apartment, leave them there and walk down to the row of restaurants across from the park where he'd first told her about her father.

They were in a little bistro that was too expensive for her and China to ever have tried despite the proximity to them, and over glasses of predinner wine, Dylan had brought up the afternoon's incident by apologizing for her having to run interference with his former fiancée.

"It was me," he confessed in answer to her response over his revelation, his handsome face pinched into a pained grimace. "And I can assure you that I do have a spine and showed it by being the one to call off the engagement—it wasn't the other way around. Although I know that's how Lara has told it from the start and usually I don't bother correcting it."

But he felt inclined to do it with her. Was that because he cared what she thought about him?

Not that that mattered…

"Well, I know you have a spine," she said. "You didn't have any problem standing your ground when you were outnumbered by battery-pack-throwing photographers on Wednesday. But really? You were engaged to—"

"Lara Humphrey," he confirmed as their cheese tray appetizer arrived.

"She said her name like I should know who she is."

"She's the only child of Swan Humphrey. He owns the HCI chain of banks."

"Okay," Abby said, but that meant nothing to her, either.

"Anyway, Lara's right, we do know a lot of the same people—that's how we met, at a Halloween party three years ago," Dylan went on.

"Was she nicer in costume?"

He laughed and Abby was glad to lighten his mood because he hadn't been himself since Lara's visit to the salon. His not-so-talkativeness and the tension she'd sensed when she'd returned to him and Lindie had held over even after Lindie left.

"She wasn't in costume but, yeah, she was nicer. That

tirade today is one of the two other sides of her that I didn't know were there until the end."

"No costume, but she's still a master of disguise?"

Another laugh. "God, it's nice to be here with you," he muttered, visibly relaxing right before her eyes. "Actually, not so much a disguise as a manipulation. She likes to work in subtle ways to churn things up. But if you break off an engagement with her then you're really in for it. She went so nuts that she was storming into work, into just about every place I went—including into GiGi's Sunday dinner—to scream and throw things and make a scene. She even took a baseball bat to my Jaguar."

Abby tried to suppress a smile over his utter astonishment at that. Apparently it was a particularly low blow to him.

"That's why your car had to be fixed this week?" she said.

"Right. And Lara is the reason I ended up going to Europe. I didn't want to take her to court and get a restraining order and make a big, public deal about it, but her constant public attacks against me needed to stop. I thought out of sight, out of mind. That maybe if I got away she'd cool off, hopefully find somebody else, and then I'd be off the hook and could just deal with the fallout I'd left behind."

"Fallout," Abby echoed. "Is that what's going on between you and your family now?"

"It's why they're not so happy with me, yeah."

"Because you broke up with her? Or because you brought her around in the first place? Or…what?" Abby asked, making the only two guesses she could come up with.

"They're unhappy with me because of what went

on *before* I broke up with her. Because of garbage she pulled with them all. And because of garbage she pulled with me and how I handled it all..." he muttered under his breath. "I don't know if it comes from Lara being an only child or what, but she did not play well with others."

Abby smiled at that, too. "Did she not like your family?" she asked as if that were unthinkable. Because to her, it was—since they'd all been so nice to both her and China. But maybe she and China were wrong.

"Honest to God, I don't have any explanation for it. Lara seemed to like them fine. She and my sisters and Jani knew each other before Lara and I hooked up. They weren't best friends, but they were all friendly whenever their paths crossed. You've met us, you've been to Sunday dinner—nothing was any different with Lara than it's been with you, so..." He shrugged. "I thought it was okay."

Their meals arrived and he stopped talking while the server was there. He started again when the server had left.

"But it seemed like Lara just had to stir things up," he went on without prompting.

"How?"

"Nasty little girl stuff—that's what GiGi called it. Lara did a lot of going between people, confiding that they weren't really liked, that someone had said something rotten about them—that kind of stupid, just mean stuff that made trouble and hurt feelings."

"So it wasn't you who was the family troublemaker, but in this case, you introduced someone into the mix who was."

"Bingo!"

"And you didn't know what she was doing?"

"I didn't. I didn't have a clue that she was riling everybody up. I knew she was kind of a gossip but I didn't know that it went *far* beyond that. I did notice that all of a sudden there was something weird going on in the ranks—"

"Like what?" Abby asked, not understanding.

"I'd really see it at Sunday dinner. One of my brothers and his wife or girlfriend would be avoiding another one of my brothers and *his* wife or girlfriend. Or one of my sisters would be really cold to one of the other girls. But I didn't think much of it—I guess I was kind of oblivious. Then Lara started with me—"

"Nasty little girl stuff?"

"More like poor-me stuff. She'd show up at my place after shopping or whatever with the girls and claim one of them had said something to her that had hurt her feelings or that had been really bitchy. And it wasn't only the girls. She claimed that Dane had made a comment about her being fat. She said that Derek snubbed her. She said that Lang had screamed at her for giving Carter a treat—"

"And they hadn't?"

"I was never there when it supposedly happened. But I hadn't ever seen anything like that go on, and it didn't sound like my family so I thought she was being oversensitive. I tried to tell her that I was sure—and I was—that no one could have meant anything because it just isn't how we are."

"That didn't appease her, though," Abby said with some authority.

"Oh, no. That just seemed to make it worse. Then she pulled out all the stops to show me they didn't like her. Which, to be honest, by then they didn't because she'd apparently been making problems with everybody for a while—telling Vonni that Jani had said something vicious about her, claiming to Gia that Lindie couldn't stand her, pretending she was doing Heddy a favor by letting her know that everybody was sick to death of her cheesecakes—"

"Ohhh, but she makes the *best* cheesecake," Abby protested because she'd tasted one of them at the Sunday dinner.

"I know. And we all love them, we're always thrilled when she brings one around, so it wasn't true. But that's the kind of below-the-belt stuff Lara was doing while pretending to be nice."

"And they were all getting upset and mad but not saying anything to you."

"Right. But they did start giving Lara a wider berth, understandably—"

"Which meant there were real slights to upset her."

He nodded. "And then there was a lot of *she said this to me*, or *she snubbed me* that was for real from Lara and she wanted me to defend her. To force my family to be nicer to her—that's what she said. I didn't want to make waves but...hell, I didn't know what to do. Like I told you, I've always been the protective type when it comes to the people who are important to me. By this point, Lara and I were engaged. I was planning to spend the rest of my life with her. And when it went on and on and she was coming to me more and more hysterical and mad and wounded..."

"You had to rescue her."

He sighed and took a drink of wine. "I cared about her and I thought I knew her. I couldn't imagine why she would say these things if they hadn't happened, couldn't figure out why my family was being so rotten to her..."

"So you stepped up to fight her battles."

"In the beginning, I tried to be diplomatic while also

saying that it really wasn't cool to tell my fiancée that she was fat, or could they try a little harder to be nice to her. You know, that kind of thing. Then Lara made a *really* big to-do with Cade's wife—I don't know if you have the roster straight, but Cade's wife, Nati, is also my grandmother's husband Jonah's granddaughter—"

"I remember."

"Well, Lara had been spreading rumors that Nati was cheating on Cade and it got back to Nati."

"Who wasn't cheating?"

"Not by a long shot. Anyway, there was a big blowup one Sunday after dinner, when it was only the family left. Everyone had had it with all this going on by then. Jonah and Cade both got mad on Nati's behalf, pretty much the whole family was anti-Lara and it showed. I had Lara hanging onto me like an abused kid, begging me to stand by her—"

"Which you felt obligated to do since you were engaged to her."

"Right. So I did, saying that I was sure there was some mistake, that Lara hadn't done anything wrong. No one was buying that and then GiGi blew a gasket and told me what had been going on that I didn't know about—including that Lara had told GiGi that I felt as if GiGi had neglected me when I was a kid." He sighed again, shook his head and both of his eyebrows arched high. "Wow, I just never thought one woman could make so much of a mess..."

Abby nodded knowingly, but just for her own sake, to make sure her impression of his family was correct, she asked, "You were sure it was her and not your family?"

"I got sure. First of all, I'd never said—or felt—as if GiGi neglected me. She didn't, plain and simple, so there was nothing I'd ever said that could possibly have led

Lara to think that—it was a flat-out lie. Then I talked to everybody else and, believe me, there was a lot of steam ready to be blown off by then. But what my family was finally saying made more sense than what Lara had been telling me. Sure, it was all 'he said, she said,' but what it came down to was what I knew of them all, so I made my own call and no, I didn't come away with any doubt that Lara was to blame. It wasn't a misunderstanding. She'd done it all deliberately. She was just a train wreck…"

Once again he shook his head, his expression relaying his disbelief even now.

"I still couldn't tell you why, what was behind any of it, but whatever it was, by the time I'd figured it out and heard everybody's story, I'd already done a lot of taking Lara's side—*against* my family—and they were just about as disgusted with me as they were with her. They hated the idea that I hadn't just *known* that they wouldn't have ever done what she accused them of. It ended up seeming like I'd turned on them, I guess."

"Ouch."

"Yeah."

"That's why you think they like me better than you right now?"

He laughed and she was once more happy to see his mood could be lightened. "Pretty much. Then I had to get away to keep her from coming at me, so I left for Europe before I'd been able to make things up to everyone, and that's what I came home to—a lot of anger and resentment that I'm trying to wade through to repair my relationships with everyone."

Abby merely raised a knowing chin as their waiter came to remove their plates and ask if they wanted dessert. They didn't, so Dylan paid the check and they left to walk back to her apartment in the cool evening air.

When they got there it just seemed as if there wasn't a question about Dylan coming in, so Abby unlocked her door and led the way, closing it after them and offering him post-dinner coffee.

"No, thanks, I'm good." He declined the drink as they both went to sit on her sofa—Dylan nearly collapsing there with one arm along the top of the back cushions as if he was spent.

"Anyway," he repeated. "Lindie and I could hear what was going on out front today and I want you to know that I appreciate that you didn't give us away, or buy in to any of what Lara was slinging or encourage her to sling more when that was what she was looking for an opening to do."

"You're welcome. But I wouldn't have done any of that regardless. I learned through experience when I was just a kid to make up my own mind about people. I've met your family and I like them. What she was saying didn't ring true."

"And I'm guessing there are a few bridezillas you deal with now, too, that aren't *un*like Lara," he said, as if he was relieved to veer from the subject of the calamity caused by his relationship.

She smiled. "A few bridezillas, yes. And now and then a bride who seems like she's getting married for revenge because all she can talk about is the ex who's going to be sorry and how awful he was. Or his mother or his sister. Those brides tend to be repeat customers."

He laughed. "I'm guessing they're repeat brides."

"And then it was Mr. Right One who turned out to be evil and awful—or his family—"

"And the next time it's Mr. Right Two who's the bad guy," Dylan added, laughing again.

"Some people have a pattern," Abby confirmed.

He reached to brush her hair away from the shoulder of the sleeveless turtleneck top she was wearing. In the process his hand barely brushed her bare skin, but it was enough to send little sparkles of pleasure through her that she tried to ignore.

"All I know," he said with a tenderness aimed at her, "is that it was really me who dodged a bullet with Lara. Thank God everything came to light before we actually got married."

"Sure. But it still must have hurt. You didn't get to the point of proposing because you didn't love her, so it couldn't have been easy or painless to break it off."

"No, it wasn't. But I'm a big boy. I can handle what I have to handle."

And why was she thinking that she'd like him to be handling her right at that minute, only in a far more literal way?

She nudged at those thoughts to get rid of them, but sitting there the way they were, looking into his handsome face in the heavy shadows of the sunset coming in through her windows, she just couldn't do it. Any more than she could make herself get up and switch on the lights to interrupt the mood that was turning quiet and intimate and oh, so nice...

Dylan was looking into her eyes with those beautiful blue ones of his and smiling a small smile that seemed full of a kind of admiration she wasn't accustomed to seeing. A kind that warmed her from the inside out.

He drew a deep breath and sighed as if he was releasing a lot of pent-up tension. "No matter what went into it, today I was grateful to you for being the wall between my family and the garbage Lara likes to throw around. I just wish I could've come out to deal with Lara on my own. But if I'd come out, it would've given away that Lindie was there and opened the door for Lara to make one of her scenes."

"It was no big deal," Abby assured.

"It was a big deal to me. And to poor Lindie—she was ready to run out the back door and hide in the van in case Lara stormed through the place to find us. I think she was worried Lara would yank those pieces of foil off her head and take her hair with it. Then she realized you were taking care of things and she didn't have to worry."

Somewhere in the middle of that his hand slipped underneath her hair to the nape of her neck where he was giving her the most wonderful massage. So wonderful that she was thinking more about his touch and how much she liked it than about what he was saying.

Then he leaned forward at the same time he used that hand to pull her toward him and kissed her. A kiss unlike any that had come before it.

There was no good-night in this one. Instead, it was slow and alluring, weaving a spell that invited her in and asked her to stay awhile. And despite the fact that she kept swearing to herself that she wasn't going to do this again, she just wanted to so much she couldn't turn down that invitation.

She moved in slightly more, all on her own, and even pressed a hand to his chest.

That chest she'd had fantasies about being up against.

And, oh, what a nice chest it was! Rock solid and strong.

His other arm came around her as his lips parted over hers, pulling her even closer and settling in to that kiss that by all indications was the beginning of a make-out session.

Abby couldn't muster any resistance to that, either, and let her other arm snake under his so she could reach around to his back, also big and broad and all man under the palm that memorized every contour of massive muscle and tendon.

Lips parted even more and his tongue came testing the waters.

It was Abby's turn to send an invitation and she did, meeting his tongue with the tip of her own, fencing with him, parrying every thrust playfully.

And play they did. With kisses that intensified and mouths that opened wide and tongues that held nothing back as time flew by. No matter how much kissing they did, it still didn't seem like enough, and every minute only whetted Abby's appetite for more.

For his hands doing things other than cradling her head or brushing her cheek or tracing the column of her neck or cupping her shoulder.

For his clothes to disappear so she could know the texture of the skin of his back, his chest, his whole body.

For her own clothes to disappear so she could be up against him, flesh to flesh, his hand the only thing to come between them as he found her naked breasts...

But it was that thought, that yearning as darkness filled her apartment and they were more sprawled on her sofa than sitting on it, that finally gave her pause.

Clothes could not *come off!* a small voice in the back of her mind shouted at her.

Hands could not go wandering any farther than the not-intimate places they already had.

And this kissing had to stop or both of those things were going to happen.

Reluctantly she pushed against that very, very fine chest of his and whispered, "Air!" as if she needed to come up for that.

He kissed her again, anyway, long and lingering and oh, so sexy, but then he stopped and just held her nestled against him, her cheek to his chest, his head resting on top of hers.

"That improved this rotten day," he said in a quiet, raspy voice.

She'd gotten to spend the afternoon looking at his reflection in her station mirror, then have dinner with him, and now this—she didn't consider it to have been a rotten day at all. Even factoring in the tantrum of his former fiancée. So she didn't say anything. She merely let herself remain a few minutes longer in his arms, drinking in the scent of his cologne and the heat he gave off.

But she was so comfortable she was afraid that if she didn't send him on his way soon she never would, so she said, "It's late."

"I know," he answered, as if he knew everything that was going through her mind. And agreed with it, but wasn't any more eager than she was to put this night behind them.

But eventually it was Dylan who found the will, because he held her so tight she really could hardly breathe for a split second and then he took her by the shoulders and sat her up and away from him as he sat straighter himself.

"Big day tomorrow," he said as he stood. "Rehearsal dinner tomorrow night. You and your team have the first lap and then I'll be at GiGi's house to take you with me."

There was something that almost sounded possessive in the way he said that. And why that gave her a flush of pleasure she didn't know. But it did.

She tried to ignore it and stood, too, going with him to her door and opening it, hoping that the exposure would keep her from doing what she was most inclined to do—just drag him back to her sofa for more kissing.

And *more* than kissing…

"Thanks for dinner," she said.

"Thanks for everything else," he countered, not touching her but leaning over to kiss her again—a deep, lingering kiss that made her feel as if she somehow belonged lip-locked with him.

Then he straightened once more, studied her face for a moment as if he needed that one last look at her, and said, "Sleep tight."

"You, too," she responded, as if there was no doubt that would follow.

But it wasn't likely.

Because she already knew that after an evening with him, closing her eyes would only bring her back to the feel of being in his arms, back to each and every detail of kissing him, to so many other things she wanted to do with him.

And sleep only took her away from the memories and the fantasies that went even further.

The memories and fantasies that she didn't want sleep to rob her of…

Chapter Eight

Abby and China and the rest of the special occasions team spent Friday afternoon doing Camden hair, makeup and nails for the rehearsal and dinner. During the course of that they were invited to attend the wedding and reception the next day.

The Camdens proposed that after the prewedding preparations, the team could get ready themselves while pictures were being taken. To help make it work for them, the Camdens were providing a limousine that would pick them all up, bring them to the family home to do their jobs, then transport them to the church, to the country club reception and take them home afterward.

It was the biggest perk the team had ever been offered and they accepted with excitement at the prospect.

Abby appreciated the gesture and a part of her wished it had extended to the rehearsal dinner that she alone was slated for. Because when everyone else left and she went to a spare room in GiGi's house to change, she started to worry that the rehearsal and dinner might be stuffy and snooty, and that she would feel out of place on her own.

She was especially nervous about it when she put on the simple black halter dress she'd brought to wear. It had a high banded waist and a plunging neckline. And with the sexy black hose and four-inch stiletto sandals that completed the outfit, she was concerned that altogether the outfit might not be appropriate for a high-society wedding rehearsal.

Her fears were unfounded, though, because the rehearsal dinner turned out to be not at all stuffy or snooty. In fact, it was more like bachelor or bachelorette parties she'd heard about.

Abby only learned on the trip between the church and the location of the rehearsal dinner that the rehearsal was being hosted by Dylan and held in the community room on the second floor of the building where his loft was located.

Beer and wine flowed freely, and dinner was a buffet of fondue stations manned by caterers who provided multiple choices for five different courses.

Dining tables lined the other three perimeters of the space that was decorated like a starry night—all in sparkling silver, white and ice blue against blackout privacy curtains that concealed the windows.

In the center of the room under mirror balls were casino-like gambling tables where dealers freely handed out foil-wrapped chocolate coins to use as chips.

Music played, muted only when a round of toasts to the bride and groom interrupted it. Then it began again and everyone returned to gambling, ignoring the option to dance in favor of the games.

Altogether, the whole thing had a festive atmosphere that was anything *but* snobby. Abby actually sat between

GiGi and Margaret for several hands of blackjack and had as much fun as she would have had playing alongside China.

Because it was the night before the wedding, the event only lasted until about ten before breaking up and leaving Abby feeling guilty.

"You should have told me a lot earlier that this was in the building where you live," she said after the last good-night. "I could have driven myself and then you wouldn't have to take me home."

"I wanted to make it easy on you. And I don't mind the drive. But would you like to see my place before we go?"

Abby was a little dismayed to note that there was nothing in that that sounded like a come-on. She had the impression that he really just wanted to show her his loft, without any ulterior motives. And the building was one of Denver's most elite and not anywhere Abby had ever been before. She was curious to see another example of how the other half lived—not to mention how Dylan lived. She was also not anxious to end the evening, so she said, "I would."

"We'll have to go back down to the first floor to get to the elevator we need to use," he informed her, thanking the staff that remained to clean and close up as he ushered Abby out of the party room.

"So how did you come to be the one in charge of the rehearsal dinner? Which, by the way was a whole lot more fun than I thought it would be—isn't it usually just a fancy dinner?" she asked as they walked.

"It is usually just a fancy dinner and I offered to do it to make *that* easy on everyone."

"As part of getting back on your family's good side?"

He nodded. "Yep."

"But isn't the rehearsal dinner supposed to be the groom's side of things?"

"It is. Traditionally. But this was kind of a unique situation. Not only was the whole wedding done in little more than a month—which made it hard to get venues—but it's Sawyer's second marriage and there's some history between his dad and our family."

"Bad history?"

"Yeah…" he admitted, as if he wished he didn't have to. "My uncle Howard—"

"The Camden cousins' father or an uncle on your mother's side?"

"Seth, Cade, Beau and Jani's dad. He did some kind of dirty dealings to distract Sawyer's father so he could snatch my aunt Tina out from under him."

"Ohhh," Abby said, raising her eyebrows at hearing some of the family dirt.

"Yeah. That made for a grudge against us that Sawyer ran with. He's become our Superstores' worst nightmare—he owns a consulting firm that goes into every area where we want to open a new store and stirs up support against us on behalf of the local businesses."

Abby raised her eyebrows higher as they went into a secluded area of the lobby to three elevators that could only be activated with keys.

"Your sister is marrying your family's arch enemy?"

"Pretty much," he confirmed with a wry laugh as he let them into an elevator. "But other than what he does for a living, Sawyer's a nice guy. Lindie loves him and he treats her well, so we all separate the man from the job. But tonight was the first time his family—particularly his father—and our family were all going to get together. So I thought it might be better to have some stuff going on rather than putting everybody at a table and expecting them to just chat."

"That seems smart," Abby said. "And it was fun."

"I'm glad you had a good time. And you're not a bad card dealer—I saw you take a turn at that blackjack table."

She laughed. "That was your grandmother and Margaret's idea—they didn't like the cards they were getting from the dealer and they were giving him a hard time. They said they wanted a new dealer and I volunteered. It's one of the sort-of skills I picked up from an older kid I was in a foster home with when I was nine."

"Somebody taught you to deal cards like a Las Vegas dealer at age nine?" he repeated with shock.

"I could lie, but yes, I was nine. The girl who taught me was fifteen and had lived in Vegas with her mother for most of her life. Her mother was a cardshark and groomed her to do the same thing by teaching her everything she knew."

"Not history or science, but how to cheat at cards?"

"Right. Then she and her mother moved here with some guy her mother met in Vegas and he abused Clair. When a beating from the boyfriend landed Clair in the emergency room and the police were called, her mom took the boyfriend's side. That's how she got into the system here. But she was nice to me—she called me her *little nugget* and I followed her around like her sidekick while we were in that foster home."

He shook his head at that story as they stepped into the elevator. "Remind me never to play poker with you."

"Chicken!" she goaded him.

Once inside the elevator Abby noticed that there were only two buttons to be pushed—an up arrow and an arrow facing down.

"Why aren't there buttons for every floor?" she asked as the doors closed and the ride began.

"Because this elevator only goes to my place."

Abby tried not to show surprise at that. "What about the other two elevators?"

"They go to the apartments one and two floors under mine."

"You have the penthouse?"

"I do."

"Oh," she muttered.

Then the elevator came to a stop and the doors opened. Right into his loft.

"There's not a hallway or a door you can lock or anything..." she observed, peering into the expansive area where she could see an elaborate kitchen, dining room and living room.

"The elevator only works with my key or if I operate it from up here for a guest."

"Nobody else lives up here?"

"I have the whole top floor."

"Oh," she repeated as more of what she was seeing and learning sank in.

And peering at the splendor of his loft from the elevator that was his alone, she suddenly felt totally out of her depth.

"Of all the places I've lived, none of them has *ever* been anything like this..."

He swept an arm out so she would leave the elevator ahead of him.

For some reason, Abby was actually hesitant to do that. A voice in her head was screaming that this was *not* a place she belonged!

But what was she going to do now that she was here?

She stepped gingerly onto the hardwood floor as if she might do damage and apparently Dylan noticed.

"Kick off your shoes, if you want. Be comfortable," he advised her.

She wondered if he thought her feet hurt, but it also occurred to her that he might not want her high heels on his flooring so she did take off her shoes, setting them with the pointed toes to the wall beside the elevator and thinking that she would never be comfortable in this place.

"Come on, I'll give you the fifty cent tour and then we can sit and relax for a bit—unless you're in a hurry to get home?"

"There's no rush," she said quietly, as if not to disturb something.

He had on a suit and tie, and off came the coat then. Next went the tie and he unfastened the collar button of his shirt and stretched his neck as if it felt good to be free of the restraint.

And while Abby enjoyed the sight as much as she always enjoyed the sight of him, somehow seeing him in this place she so obviously didn't belong tempered the enjoyment a bit.

"Come on," he said, taking her hand as he showed her the three bedrooms, four bathrooms, workout room and office that went with the kitchen, living and dining rooms.

Along the way he deposited his coat and tie on the bed in the master suite and then he took her back to the living room.

"Can I get you something?" he asked, nodding at the kitchen.

"No, thanks, I took a few too many trips to the chocolate fountain so I'm done for the day."

"Then let's sit," he suggested, spinning her like a dance partner to the front of the white leather sectional sofa that formed a large U around the biggest tufted white leather ottoman she'd ever seen.

"So, what do you think about the digs?" he asked when she'd let herself be swallowed up by one corner of the couch and he sat at an angle beside her.

"Nice?" she said uncertainly. "I mean, what do you say about a place like this? It's right out of a magazine or a movie or something. And you *live* here? By yourself?"

"All by my lonesome. Not like the way I grew up, either—I mean, sure, GiGi's house is huge and spectacular and in demand every time Denver wants to do showings of the most noteworthy homes. But GiGi didn't have enough rooms for each of us to have one alone, so growing up we always had to share. First year of college I was in a dorm—more sharing. Then an apartment with roommates—more sharing bathrooms and the kitchen, even if I had a bedroom to myself. So, yeah, sometimes it feels weird even to me to have this whole place to myself."

He unfastened his cuff links, tossed them carelessly onto the ottoman and proceeded to roll both sleeves to just below his elbows.

Abby enjoyed watching his hands, seeing his wrists and forearms slowly exposed.

But again, like seeing him remove his coat and tie, it somehow felt as if she shouldn't be ogling him here.

"How about you?" he asked then. "Did you ever have a room to yourself?"

"A few times," she said as he finished with his sleeves and stretched both arms out along the top of the sofa back, sprawled magnificently. "Sometimes the reason people take in a foster kid is because they have a spare room."

"So you weren't always with a bunch of other foster kids?"

Hoping to find a way to feel more comfortable—and since she didn't have shoes on—she curled her legs up to the side and tucked her feet under her skirt.

"Usually I was, but sometimes I was the only one in a home."

"How many homes were you in?"

She laughed mirthlessly. "I couldn't possibly have kept track—remember, I started in the system when I was two."

"That's so little. They couldn't find you an adoptive family?"

"Two is little. But it's still old for people wanting to adopt. Most of them want babies—newborns especially, or, at least, the newer the better."

"So they just moved you around over and over again?"

"I was always in flux, yes. A good run was being in the same place for a year."

"And otherwise it was less than that?" he asked in astonishment.

"Most of the time it was less than that."

"Why?"

She shrugged. "All sorts of people take in foster kids for all sorts of reasons. Some of the reasons, and the people, are genuinely good and giving and generous and caring. Some of the reasons, and the people, are not so great. Sometimes it's just for the money. Sometimes the foster parents imagine that it will be a certain way and don't like what it really is—"

"Which is what?"

"Taking strangers into your home who can have bad

attitudes or be troubled or difficult. And who are, one way or another, still *kids*—messy and rambunctious and not always obedient or well-mannered or…nice. And if the foster parent has gone into it to have their own need to be loved or adored met, they can get disappointed fast and change their minds."

Abby shrugged again. "And everything changes all the time—funding, regulations, the families themselves if they move or divorce or lose jobs or get better jobs somewhere else. Or something can change with their own kids, or they don't have kids of their own and then decide to. Or if their own kids develop issues themselves or just get old enough to go off to college and the foster parents decide they want to be free of all kids. There are a million reasons."

"Did you just live on edge all the time, never knowing how long you'd be in one place?"

"I wouldn't say I was on edge. I just always knew that wherever I was, it probably wasn't for long. Living the way I did was just what I knew. Even when I had drawers or a closet to put my things in, I still left most of my stuff in my suitcase—that was like my portable home—and then if I got taken away without warning I could just zip it up and go without risking that I'd leave behind something I'd miss."

He scrunched his eyes closed as if he couldn't bear what she was saying. "No!" he said more forcefully. "The only way this could be worse was if you had to pack a trash bag with your stuff."

"There are a lot of stories worse than mine," she assured him. "I was never abused or molested or anything. And I actually did use a trash bag until I asked for a suitcase for Christmas and got it."

His eyes were open again and his brow was beetled

forlornly over them. "So you made the best of it, but I gotta tell you—still sad." He shook his head and, as if he was searching for a positive note, said, "When did you meet China?"

"When we were both fifteen we landed in the same foster home. That particular one wanted free labor—we were nannies to their real kids, and we were responsible for the cooking, cleaning, laundry—"

"Did that happen a lot?"

"It wasn't a surprise," she said with a laugh. "Some foster families see it as a perk of taking in older kids when they have little ones of their own. It isn't a bad thing. China and I got to be friends doing it. But about eight months into it the dad was transferred for work. China and I were old enough by then to go into group housing so we opted for that if we could stay together. It was the first genuine friendship I'd had."

"Oh, just when I think you can't get to me again," he groaned in mock pain. "China was your first real friend at *fifteen*?"

Abby confirmed that with a shrug. "I moved around a lot—that meant changing schools most of the time. I wasn't really able to join clubs or sports teams, and it wasn't usually an option for me to go to birthday parties or sleepovers, so it was hard to get close to my classmates. As for the other kids in my house, I didn't always like them. They didn't always like me. Mark wasn't wrong that I was in close quarters with troubled kids, with troublemaker kids. I knew some kids like your ex who would cause me problems or could be an actual danger to me if I got too close. And maybe the difference, too, was that I was older when I met China. We were teenagers—when you really feel like no one understands you except someone your own age. When *everyone* else is annoying and uncool."

"Did you and China stay in the same group home after that?"

"We stayed together, but our location moved a few times. There were four group homes—neighborhoods tend not to be happy to have them in their area and do what they can to get them shut down. Or something in the system changes and they close. But our caseworkers liked us and they knew we were good together, that neither of us was a bad kid and that we both just wanted to graduate high school and were sort of bolstering each other to do that. So they made sure we stayed together. I don't think it was easy, but they did it."

"That was nice."

"Like I said, not everything was bad," Abby reasserted. "It just was what it was. When we graduated and aged out of the system we got a really tiny apartment together so we could make rent. Neither of us were making enough money for separate apartments even after we finished cosmetology school so we went on being roommates—actually until I moved in with Mark."

"Then that ended and you stayed with China again."

It was nice that he was attentive enough to really listen and remember what she told him.

"And then the apartment I'm in now opened up, and by then we could both swing our own rent, so I moved across the hall."

"Have you always worked together?"

"No. We've overlapped at a few salons, worked at different ones some of the time. China came to Beauty By Design when I started the special events stuff. She was working at another salon then, but I knew she wanted to do more makeup than hair and was really good at it, so I talked her into moving."

He nodded. "And in all of that, what experience did you have that taught you to make up your own mind about people—like you told me last night? How many spoiled brats like Lara could there have been?"

Abby laughed at that. "It wasn't that there were spoiled brats. But there were all kinds of kids. And parents. And kids of parents. I learned early to try to stay out of the *nasty little girl stuff.*"

"What GiGi called what Lara did."

"Right. I was about six the first time I went into a home and one of the other girls my age became my instant best friend. She told me all kinds of bad things about the other two foster kids who lived there and really scared me away from them. She said that she and I should stick together. I fell for it, thought I'd better steer clear of the other kids and that I was lucky that I had Nessa. Until one morning I got up and found that Nessa had told the other kids how bad *I* was and tried to get everybody against me."

"Ooo, that *does* sound like Lara."

"You meet all kinds growing up the way I did, so you have to learn to make your own call about people."

"And you have to be resilient," he said, as if it was something he was adding to a list of her accomplishments.

Abby laughed again. "You have to be resilient just to get through life, don't you?"

"Not all lives—most of them are not like yours."

Mark had said things similar to that. But he'd said them with such horror. When he said it, it meant that he wanted what her early life had entailed to be swept under the rug. Somehow when Dylan said it, it made her sound admirable for having weathered it.

And even though she still didn't feel totally comfortable in the posh, sophisticated surroundings she was in, she discovered that she once more felt comfortable with him.

Especially with those blue, blue eyes looking at her the way they were, oblivious to everything *but* her, and making her aware of only him, too.

"You're kind of remarkable—do you know that?" he said in a dark whiskey voice.

"I'm really not," she responded quietly.

Something about that made him smile just before he slipped a hand through her hair to the back of her head and came in for a kiss.

Abby's eyes drifted shut and then it didn't matter where they were. All that mattered was that his mouth was pressed to hers because nothing seemed more right than that.

He toyed with her a bit, kissing her with his head tilted in one direction, breaking away to kiss her with his head tilted in the other direction. Slow kisses that savored the moment and her. Leisurely kisses that began and ended and began again, drawing her in, playful and sexy and alluring and inviting.

Which was how Abby answered them, welcoming it when the kisses grew longer, deeper. Parting her lips when he parted his. Happy when his tongue darted in and disappeared back out again only to dart in once more and make her secretly smile at his games.

His other arm went around her and he slid her to him. He pulled her so close to him that it wouldn't have taken much more for her to be on his lap. But that wasn't where she ended up. Instead, with her feet still tucked under her hip, her knees rested on his left thigh.

One of her hands raised to the side of his neck—thick and warm—while her other rested against his chest, savoring the feel of that wall of steel again, massaging it slightly as she felt her nipples tighten and begin to yearn for a little attention.

Their mouths were wider by then, the kisses less playful and more passionate.

The hand that cradled her head dropped to her nape where a knot kept the halter dress's top up.

*Go ahead...untie it...*she thought.

But he only fiddled with it for a moment before he did something even better—he hooked his fingers underneath it and used it as a guide over her shoulder, past her collarbone, down the upper portion of her chest to the very first swell of her breast—bare beneath the dress because the cut of the neckline made a bra impossible.

He stopped there, tantalizing her with that pause just when she thought he was going to go lower.

Tease! she mentally shouted at him, giving him a taste of his own medicine by letting her legs move up his thigh just enough to reach his zipper.

He squirmed slightly and his hand slid farther down, letting only the backs of his fingers brush her bare nipple at first and making her do a little squirming herself.

Until he did what she was really wishing for—he took her breast fully into his palm from outside of the strip of fabric that covered it.

It felt so good she expanded into that hand, her nipple a hard pebble responding all on its own to his touch, yearning for more, for there to be no fabric at all between them.

Kissing had turned heated and filled with all new

cravings then. Cravings that did drive his hand under her dress and made her whisper-moan with that initial feel of skin on skin.

Big and capable, that glorious hand of his kneaded and massaged and caressed. There was play and teasing in that, too, for a time, before it became more. Before his fingers pressed into her flesh as if he couldn't get enough of the feel of her, gently nipping and tenderly pinching and testing the tautness of that pebble of nipple, too.

Up a little higher on his leg went her knees. High enough to let her know that she wasn't the only one of them getting more turned on by the minute.

He had a big bed in that bedroom he'd shown her...

After last night she'd thought about where this was going. Where she wanted it to go and just how far she was willing to let it go. And she'd sort of made a decision.

She didn't have any illusions about Dylan the way she'd had about Mark. So she knew there was no future with Dylan.

But there was still right now.

And if she kept her eyes wide-open, if she kept in mind that it would all be over with after tomorrow night's wedding, if she didn't expect anything real or fool herself into thinking it was more than a lark, she thought that maybe she could let herself enjoy this— him—while it lasted.

And let later just be later.

Only tonight was a little different. Even if she *had* decided she could just roll with whatever happened between them, somehow the thought of going further in this place where she felt so strongly that she didn't belong put a damper on things.

And tomorrow was his sister's wedding. Abby knew that Dylan had an early golf game with all of the other male members of the Camden family. She knew that was to be followed by last-minute wedding errands, and then dressing and getting to the church.

She had a full, full day for that same wedding. So if she let this go where her entire body was urging her, it would mean a predawn frenzy to follow so that they could both get on with the day ahead. A predawn frenzy in this sterile place that didn't feel anything like home to her.

And that felt as if it might cheapen what she didn't want to be cheap in any way.

That was why, after indulging in his skip to her other breast and letting his magic hand work even more wonders there for a little while as he rained kisses and sexy little tip-of-his-tongue flicks against the side of her neck, she said, "You should take me home."

The problem was, it didn't sound as if she meant it.

Probably because he was awakening things inside of her that were so much stronger than common sense.

So for some time longer they went on kissing and he went on tantalizing her breasts, and somewhere along the way her knees rose all the way to such an impressive bulge in his suit pants...

Until she knew it was now or never and, forcing more oomph into her voice, she said, "Really...you need to take me home. Tomorrow is a crazy day for us both."

He kissed her again and almost every resolve dwindled under the pure heat of it that melted what little resistance to him she had.

But then he ended the kiss, sighed and said, "I honestly didn't bring you up here to seduce you."

She knew that. This was just always what seemed to ignite when they were together.

But tonight it had to stop here.

He took a deep breath, exhaled, closed his eyes, and seemed to be forcibly regaining some control.

Then he clasped her hand in his and got them both to their feet.

"Home," he said as if he needed a refresher course in what he was doing.

"Bet now you're wishing you'd let me drive myself over here tonight," she teased.

"Uh-uh," he insisted. "It's gonna take some fresh air and the drive back alone if there's any hope of sleeping tonight."

Neither of them had much beyond small talk to exchange on the ride down the elevator or on the drive to her place. But he did seem to have some problems not touching her because he held her hand all the way to his car and, even as he maneuvered the quiet streets that took them just outside of Denver, he kept reaching over to squeeze her knee or to brush the backs of his fingers against her cheek or to massage her neck.

Then they were at her place, where he again held her hand as he walked her to her door, swinging her to face him when they reached it so he could kiss her again—intensely enough that she knew he hadn't yet cooled down.

"Tomorrow," he said when he seemed to access his own willpower sufficiently to end that kiss and finally take his hands completely off her.

"Big day," she said.

"Big day," he repeated.

And their last day together, Abby thought.

But somehow she knew that the wedding wouldn't be where their last day actually ended.

That that wasn't likely to come until what had been stirred up between them tonight found a conclusion of its own.

After that wedding was over...

Chapter Nine

"Hey! Nice party last night, man!"

"Yeah, but next time can we play with real money? I had a whole pile of winnings I just had to *eat*."

"But let's keep the same system where Dylan has to bankroll us all."

"I second that!"

Everyone laughed at the volley of words that came Dylan's way from Dane, Lang and Derek when his brothers spotted him coming into GiGi's kitchen early Saturday morning.

It was Lindie's wedding day and his entire family plus wives, fiancés and kids were gathered at his grandmother's house for the kind of breakfast they'd all shared growing up there.

But Dylan stopped short in the kitchen doorway. Since the Lara debacle he'd become accustomed to entering occasions with his family and having them all act as if they hadn't noticed. This morning, for the first time in months, not only was his arrival being noted, he was being greeted. Cheerfully. And he wasn't sure how to act.

It had been a long while since he'd had a reception like that. This was the kind of teasing and warmth he would have been met with at any other time pre-Lara. Not only did it surprise him, it choked him up a little.

GiGi paused in front of him, en route to the refrigerator, and whispered, "Looks like you've made your way back." Then she kissed him on the cheek and in a voice everyone could hear, she said, "Well, come in and help yourself—the food's all on the island, grab a plate and fill it."

"Glad everyone had a good time," Dylan said somewhat belatedly as he stepped into the kitchen, hiding how thrilled he was that his family wasn't giving him the cold shoulder any longer.

"Even the Huffmans did," Lindie said, referring to her soon-to-be in-laws. "It was a perfect way to get us all in the same room without anyone toting along any baggage. Sawyer's parents love to gamble so it gave them the chance to leave all the bad blood of the past behind and just let loose like we were all one big happy family. Thank you for that, Dylan," his sister said, sounding sincerely grateful.

"My pleasure," Dylan answered, going to the island counter laden with platters of food.

"Good job," Margaret quietly commended him as she handed him a plate, winking at him to let him know she wasn't praising him for the rehearsal dinner but for having finally appeased his family.

"Thanks," he muttered to the woman who had been his surrogate mother.

As he took a spoonful of scrambled eggs, Lindie said, "The only bad thing about last night was that I was too busy to talk to Abby. I wanted to thank her for what she did at the salon—did Dylan tell you all about that?"

Dylan froze with the eggs only halfway to his plate.

Don't do it...don't even say Lara's name...he silently beseeched his sister, worrying that any reminder of his former fiancée would stir things up again.

"Sawyer didn't get to come for breakfast?" he said to his sister to distract her.

"He can't see the bride before the wedding," Livi informed him.

That was as much as his distraction bought him before Lindie went on to outline Abby's encounter with his former troublemaking fiancée. Her story included how stressed out she'd been waiting in that back room, certain that at any moment Lara would charge through the place and cause a scene. She also painted Abby as her hero for not caving in.

While she talked Dylan finished serving himself but braced for the impact he was sure the tale would have, scanning the kitchen for a free corner where he could take his food to eat and stay out of the way if the tides turned on him again.

But his second surprise of the morning was that the worst didn't happen. Instead, when Lindie wrapped up her recounting, his grandmother's husband, Jonah, said, "Now *that's* a girl to bring into the family—one who protects you from the wolf at the door."

"And can do hair," Jani chimed in with a laugh.

"And deal cards," GiGi contributed with some humor of her own. "We had fun with her last night, didn't we, Margaret?"

"We did," the old family friend confirmed. "And she *can* do hair—even Louie likes my new do, don't you?"

"Like goin' to bed with another woman," answered

the man who had begun as the Camdens' groundskeeper and handyman.

"Good for you!" Seth said lasciviously, patting the elderly man's back while everyone laughed and Dylan wondered if he really was out of the doghouse once and for all.

When the laughter at Seth's joke died down, Jonah returned to praising Abby. "That girl seems to have her feet on the ground. I like that."

There was a general muttering of agreement.

"I think Dylan likes that, too," his cousin Beau goaded him, slightly under his breath but still loud enough for the room to hear.

"He says he's not ready to get into anything yet," Seth replied, defending him. "But when you are," he added, directing his words to Dylan, "you could do worse."

"He has done worse. *Waaay* worse," Lang said. But again only good-naturedly.

And then something seemingly minor happened that was a very big deal to Dylan—room was made for him to sit in the enormous breakfast nook.

It was the first time since Lara that he wasn't kept on the outside of things.

He knew he was grinning like an idiot but he couldn't help it as he took his breakfast and slid into the nook, feeling as if he was finally sliding back into his place in the family, too.

The taunts continued, but he was actually glad to be the recipient of them because they were vastly better than the cold shoulder he'd been getting for what seemed like so long now.

But despite this being a pivotal moment for him with his family there seemed to still be one thing missing.

Abby.

He was wishing like mad that she was with him right then to share this pivotal moment.

Ready or not...

"That was the *most* beautiful wedding I've ever seen," Abby told Dylan as he held the passenger door of his Jaguar open for her and she got in.

He closed the door and went around the front of the car to the driver's side. She let her gaze follow him the whole way because she just couldn't seem to get enough of the sight of him dressed in that tuxedo, looking better than any James Bond ever had.

It was nearly eleven o'clock on Saturday night. The rest of the special occasions team had left in the limousine provided by the Camdens. But Abby had stayed to help Lindie undo the elaborate basket weave that had made the back of her hair the centerpiece for a veil that fell from pearls encircling it. There were flowers intricately entwined throughout and it was all held together with an array of hidden hairpins.

Abby was proud of the work she'd done and how striking it had looked, but she understood that needing the groom's help taking it apart would not make for a romantic beginning to a wedding night. So she'd agreed to dismantle it for Lindie before she left. But Lindie had wanted to stay at her own reception right to the end.

Not that Abby minded. She'd loved every minute of attending that wedding and reception—the cathedral ceremony, the country club reception in a ballroom of chandeliers, white linen, cut crystal and flowers galore with food and champagne aplenty.

She'd loved being treated like part of the Camden family—because not only had they all embraced the entire special occasions team as if they were old friends,

Dylan had kept her by his side throughout the reception, which had actually made her a part of the inner circle.

And for this one night—knowing that it *was* only for this one night—she'd let herself live the fantasy and feel like Cinderella at the ball, like she belonged.

So, no, she hadn't minded staying to play that out right to the end.

And because Dylan had persuaded her to let him take her home rather than going back in the limo, the extension of the job gave her an excuse for it.

Along with an excuse to get some time alone with him.

Opening the driver's side door, he tossed his tuxedo coat, cummerbund and tie into the space behind the seat and then got in himself.

"It was a beautiful wedding," he agreed.

"And the music and the dancing and the funny toasts and that cake that was too good to be *wedding* cake with that custard stuff between the layers and…" She sighed. "It was all just amazing!"

Dylan smiled at her as he started the engine. "How much champagne have you had?"

"A lot. Not too much—I'm not drunk or anything—"

"But you also aren't feeling any pain," he finished for her.

She grinned back at him, appreciating the sight of that face that was just too handsome for her to believe sometimes.

"Actually, I *am* feeling pain. These shoes are killing me!" she confessed, taking off the four-inch-high heels she'd been in for hours and hours. But they'd looked so perfect with the dress she'd found on sale—a dark blue rayon number with elbow-length sleeves and a satin sash separating the loose knee-length skirt from the tight-fitting bodice with the neckline that scooped from barely an inch over one shoulder to barely an inch over the other.

Her hair was again full and free, and she laid her head against the headrest, turning to look only at Dylan as he headed out of Cherry Creek in the direction of her apartment.

"And what about you?" she asked then.

"I'm sober as a judge. One glass of champagne early on for the toasts is all the booze I had."

"No, I mean what about you tonight—everybody likes you again!"

That brought an instant grin to his handsome face to let her know how happy he was about it.

"Happened this morning," he said. "Don't ask me how or why or if there was some kind of secret meeting where they all decided to finally let me off the hook, but I went to breakfast over at GiGi's and it was like old times."

"Congratulations! I'm so happy for you!" She rejoiced, knowing how important making up with his family had been to him.

They were at a stoplight and he looked over at her with a smile that was warm enough for her to feel. "I'm giving you some of the credit."

"Me? You've been bending over backward for everyone. What did I do except my job?"

"Getting you to do your job on such short notice got me points. Then you—and your whole team—doing such a tremendous job got me more points. But there's something about you and having you around that softened the edges or something. I think it helped them stop looking at me as the turncoat they thought I'd become with Lara and made them start to see me as plain old Dylan again. Thanks for that."

"Well, you're welcome but I really didn't do anything."

"You were you—without any airs or ulterior motives. You went the extra mile for everyone, for this whole wedding. And this morning Lindie told them all about you running interference with Lara when she came to the salon—you may not think that was a big deal, but after what we went through with her it meant a lot to everyone and won't be forgotten. I think Jonah wants to adopt you."

"Ah, just twenty-eight years too late!" she joked.

They were well on their way to her place and he took his eyes off the road long enough to glance at her. "We all do want to do something more for you, though. We just can't let all your talent go to waste working for someone else—"

Abby made a face. "Don't go there again—I'm not going to work for your Superstores." And she didn't want to get into that subject now when she'd just had a night of feeling like she fit in, like a part of that perfect family.

"How about two other things, then? How about we hire you as a consultant—just to have meetings with Jani and Lindie and Livi to talk them through how to improve our salons? It'll be casual, just the four of you girls, and we'll pay you a consulting fee. And then how about you let us set you up in one of your own salons like Beauty By Design? With your own special occasions team? We'll make it so that you own everything outright—whatever buildings you need, whatever equipment. Your own shop where everything you do will only be benefiting you and your future, not whoever Sheila is."

Abby had thought she'd had just enough champagne to be really mellow and relaxed. Now she wondered if she'd had too much to drink to hear straight.

"Sheila's been good to me." She defended her boss because she didn't know what else to say.

"I know. We're not asking you to do anything that would hurt her. Maybe she'd be interested in selling out to you—we could set you up that way, too. You could buy her out of both shops and the special events salon. Then she wouldn't have you as competition, and you could go on doing what you do now, with the team you have in place, in the locations you're familiar with and like. Except *you* would be the owner."

Sheila *was* in her sixties and had been talking about retiring…

But this was crazy, Abby told herself. Maybe she'd had so much to drink that she'd passed out or fallen asleep and she was hallucinating or dreaming or something.

"Come on…" she cajoled in disbelief. "You're joking."

"I'm dead serious, Abby. About both things. If you won't just come to work for us as an executive, then at least be our consultant. And even when we implement improvements in our salons, we'd still throw you all of Camden Superstores' special events work because your setup offers our customers that whole party-like experience that our facilities can't. We'll work up some kind of posters to put in the wedding and fancy dress wear departments advertising you, and you can put *Recommended by Camden Superstores* in your plugs for your special occasions team."

"What's the catch?" she demanded.

He smiled. "I know you think you sound street-tough

when you use that tone of voice, but it's too cute to be intimidating." He sobered and then said, "No catch. I came looking for you to tell you who your father was and connect you with your past, but also to compensate you however we could for H.J.'s part in the twist your life took. That's all this is."

She and China had always talked about owning their own shop one day. Working for themselves. But it always seemed like just another of their fantasies—a what-if-they-won-the-lottery thing. And just as far-fetched.

"You're talking about a *lot* of money that I don't know if I could ever repay," she said.

"No repaying anything. It would come as a grant, free and clear. And we'd pay you a fee for the consulting—just money in the bank for services rendered, the same as a haircut or a color, only this would be you selling us your ideas. Just over lunch with the girls or something else simple. When it's over and we have the knowledge we need, you just walk away and do your own thing the way you like."

He pulled up in front of her apartment house and turned off the car while she continued to stare at him.

Then she shook her head and said, "I had too much champagne to talk about this."

He nodded. "No more talking about it tonight. But you can still think about it—just tell me you will."

"I will," she vowed, wondering if this was too good to be true.

But just agreeing to think about it seemed to be the only answer Dylan wanted right then because he got out of the car and came around to her side again as she fumbled on the floor to find her shoes.

She had no intention of putting them on, so when he

opened her door and she stepped out it was in nylon-encased feet.

Seeing that, Dylan bent over and scooped her up as if she weighed nothing.

"What are you doing?" she asked, grabbing him around the neck for balance while holding her shoes in one hand by their slingbacks.

"I don't want your feet to get dirty."

"You'll give yourself a hernia!"

He laughed. "I'll risk it," he said as if he wasn't worried.

"Oh, now you're just showing off," she claimed as he carried her up to the house, onto the porch, through the front door and up the flight of stairs to her apartment.

He didn't set her down until they were in front of her door.

Abby unlocked it and opened it, but didn't go in or invite him in. Even though she was definitely thinking about it...

She tossed her shoes in, though.

And then looked up into those knock-'em-dead blue eyes as he took both of her hands in his and held them loosely down at their sides.

There was something about that that was more heady than the champagne as she gazed into his so-gorgeous face. "I really did have one of the best times I've ever had," she told him.

His smile was small and thoughtful. "I'm glad. And I really did like having you there."

"You didn't need a buffer tonight," she reminded him.

His smile erupted into a grin and then calmed again. "I *still* really did like having you there," he insisted. "In fact, this morning, when the tides turned for me, I kept wishing you were there, too, to be a part of it. And," he said, his voice slightly lower, "because I just like having you around."

It was her turn to smile, treasuring the words, the sentiment, but not taking any of it too seriously. She hadn't had *so* much champagne that she was out of touch with reality or forgetting that after tonight everything would change.

And there was actually some comfort in that for her. In knowing that she would be firmly back in her place in the world—where she belonged. The place she knew the pitfalls of trying to leave behind. And that he would be firmly back in his, where he belonged and was now welcome again.

That was how it should be. It was how everything worked best. Mark had cured Abby of the illusion that life could be different.

But she still had tonight—she was very well aware of that, too. She'd been thinking about it since Dylan had left her on this very spot last night, and had gotten just a little turned on every time it had crossed her mind.

She still had tonight…

One last night with this man who made her feel the way no one else ever had. This man she wanted to fully experience. Needed to fully experience. Her own tiny special event to cherish when she looked back on it.

He was going to kiss her—she could see it in the sparkle of those fantastic eyes and she was so in tune with him that she just knew.

It caused her to tip her chin up a scant moment before he dipped down to her, to lay those sweet, supple lips to hers in a kiss that was familiar now. A kiss that allowed their mouths to fit together the way they did so well, both of his hands still holding both of hers at their sides.

She was determined to savor every single moment

of this night, to burn the memory of them all into her brain. Beginning now.

So she focused solely on that kiss. On how his lips felt against hers. On the warm brush of his breath against her cheek. On the scent of his cologne. On how his head swayed ever so slightly and how he knew when the exact right time was to let his lips part over hers. On how there was just enough invitation, just enough encouragement, just enough insistence for hers to part, too.

Then he ended the kiss as if he thought maybe this was only going to be a good-night at her door and the fact that he would have accepted that humbly, without complaint or any sense he was entitled to more, made her smile.

"Want to come in?" she asked him.

He grinned. "Oh, yeah."

"It's not like your place, though, you know. You've seen it—it's not…uptown…"

"Do you want to go back to my place?"

"No!" she said too quickly, too forcefully.

"You don't like my place?"

"It's just…not me."

"Well, it's you I want, so if this is where I find it, I'm good with that."

He had to know that there was no bedroom because he'd been there before. Her bed was on one side of the same room that was her living room, kitchen and dining area. The only separation came in the two steps up to a raised platform holding her bed and dresser.

But at least he knew what he was getting. With her, too, she thought, because unlike with Mark, Dylan knew everything there was to know about her.

Which was even more freeing than the little buzz the champagne had left her with.

So, keeping hold of his hands, she took three steps backward, into her apartment.

Without any hesitation, he came, too. And kicked the door shut behind them.

Abby took one of her hands out of his and closed the gap between them to reach around to lock the door. "China and I go back and forth if the doors aren't locked."

He nodded in understanding, took her hand back into his and kissed her again, this kiss more playful and definitely sexier as his tongue came to tantalize.

And that was that. No more conversation, no more questions. Just the two of them indulging in each other with mouths practicing the kissing they'd gotten so good at.

Dylan wrapped her in his arms then, one hand splayed to her back, the other in her hair, cupping her head.

Abby's arms curled under his so she could lay her hands to the solid expanse of his back, enjoying the thought that before long she was going to get something she'd been fantasizing about for so long—to see him without his shirt, to feel his skin and all those muscles that shirt masked.

It was such a delicious thought, such delicious anticipation, that she almost smiled under the onslaught of kissing that was growing hungrier and more demanding by the minute.

And not only was she going to get to see his bare chest, his bare back and shoulders and biceps and belly, she was going to get to see the rest of him, too…

Just the idea made her tingle all over.

Or maybe that had something to do with the kiss. And the massage he was giving her back, her side, the outer swell of the breast that was bound in the strapless bra that the wide scoop neck of her dress had required.

As much as she was enjoying the thought of things to come, she wanted it all too much to put it off, so she tugged his shirttails free of his tuxedo slacks and slipped her hands under them to finally get the first part—the feel of him.

Hot and sleek and even more solid and unyielding than she'd imagined—he had muscles to spare, explaining why he'd been able to carry her in from the car without much effort.

She let her palms learn every smooth, silky inch of that back, of his broad shoulders. Every mound of muscle, every sinew and curve. Every rib that drew her down to the narrowing of his waist and the small of that glorious back where his waistband barred her progression.

Or sent her on a detour, anyway.

Around his sides to his washboard abs.

Up again to a rock-wall of pectorals. With taut male nibs telling her that he liked her touch.

He carefully slid the zipper of her dress down then, taking her arms from under his shirt so it could glide off her shoulders into a little heap around her ankles. That left her in her lacy strapless bra, her thigh-high nylons, her thong. In the room lit only by moonlight because it hadn't occurred to her to turn on a lamp.

But the loss of her dress didn't raise any kind of inhibitions, it only seemed to provide her with license to unbutton his crisp, pleated white shirt as mouths and tongues still played.

As soon as she had the shirt open she again snaked her hands under it, this time from the front, letting palms ride the rise and swell of his chest up to his shoulders and down extraordinary biceps to send the shirt to the floor to join her dress.

There was some frenzy in their kissing then, as he

found both breasts hiding within the foam cups of her bra. He wasted no time on ceremony and unhooked it, flinging it away so he could take her bare breasts in both hands.

Ohhh, it felt so good that Abby couldn't help moaning quietly and rolling her shoulders just a little under the touch of big, adept hands that filled themselves with her, giving her nipples the perfect cove into which to tighten and nestle and nudge for some attention.

But before that happened, his hands were gone again, and Abby could feel the backs of them at her waist as he unfastened his pants.

He took something from his pocket just before he dropped trou and whatever was under them, and—unable to wait another moment—Abby reached around and grabbed the bare derriere she'd been stealing glimpses of.

Oooo, very nice! Tight and round and just right.

But she only got a split second to take that tour before he stopped kissing her and swept her up into his arms again the way he had outside, taking her to her double bed.

He tossed her onto the center of her fluffy comforter. Then he went to her nightstand to deposit the condoms he'd taken from his pants pocket.

The milky glow of streetlights coming in through the window over her bed gave Abby the chance to devour the sight of a man even more magnificent naked than she'd imagined.

There just wasn't a flawed inch of him, crowned impressively by the proof that he wanted her as much as she wanted him.

He didn't come onto the bed with her, though—the way she was yearning for him to. He went to the foot of it and stared down, getting his fill of looking at her, smiling his approval in a wicked grin as he very slowly rolled her hose down first one leg, then the other. Following with her thong so that she was as naked as he was.

Only then did he join her on the bed, crawling onto it with clear intent until his mouth recaptured hers in a kiss so sexy it felt like an unveiling of the intimacy their bodies were headed for.

He stretched out alongside her as he plundered her mouth with his, and again found her breasts with a hand that was tenderly forceful now, that took control, kneading and squeezing and gently pinching and twisting and circling diamond-hard nipples, arousing her more and more by the second.

His thigh was over hers and she let her hand travel along that muscular weight to his hip where she drew feather-light fingertips forward until she found the long, steely length of him and enclosed him in a firm grip.

He moaned his pleasure, his mouth leaving hers to kiss a path downward, replacing his hand at her breast to take her into that warm velvet that her own mouth knew so well. Sucking and nipping and nibbling, showing her more of the talents of that tongue that flicked against the sensitive kerneled crest.

Her back came slightly off the mattress in response, her spine arched and his hand followed the flat curve of her stomach to drop into the valley between her legs.

She gained a new appreciation for the size of those hands then. And his abilities, too, as he raised the level of desire and need in her.

Then he was gone, using one of those condoms from the nightstand before he was back again. Settling between her welcoming thighs, bearing his weight on outstretched arms with his hands on either side of her head, he lowered his mouth to hers once again and, at the same time, came into her in one lithe movement that made it seem as if he was just coming home.

Home to a body built especially for him to embed himself in. A body that greeted and received him as if he alone was what it was meant for.

Abby clasped her arms around his back and urged him down onto her, not caring that kissing gave way when so much more was happening.

She raised her knees to wrap her legs around his waist, her calves pulling him as deeply into her as she could manage. And then she found the rhythm of each thrust, of each retreat, of each returning glory that was the movement of him into her, of her taking him inside.

With each thrust growing increasingly more powerful and swift, they found harmony in every rise and fall of bodies striving together, working in unison, aiming for the peak of it all.

That divine peak that—when Abby reached it—exploded within her like nothing she'd ever known before and transported her somewhere outside of herself to an ecstasy so blissful she never wanted to come back.

Hanging on to that, to him, she just let wave after wave carry her in its wet, wild embrace until everything in her was spent and depleted and she couldn't hang on to it any longer, until it began to slip away from her with promises to come again.

Until the feel of Dylan plunging into the depths of her in a climax of his own made her want to relish every moment of that as much as she'd wanted to savor everything else from the very beginning of this.

So she gave herself over to that, to him, holding him tightly with fingers that dug into his back and thighs that cradled him, all while he found that same paradise in her.

Then everything slowed and slowed some more.

Except breathing that took another minute to catch up before it slowed, too.

All of Dylan's weight settled onto her. Her legs fell from around him. And for a while that was how they lingered. Peaceful. Satiated. Contentedly one.

Abby felt as if she could stay that way forever. More, she *wanted* to stay that way forever, with him inside of her.

With him never letting go of her.

Then Dylan raised his upper half and looked down at her.

"Okay...wow!"

She knew her smile was likely too big to conceal anything, but pretended indifference anyway and said, "You college boys and all your fancy words."

He grinned a weary grin. "*Wow* says it all. That was... wow."

He kissed her as if to convince her, made a very quick trip to her tiny bathroom then returned to lie on his side, pulling her to him and keeping her tightly up against him with those strong arms around her and one thigh that pulled her in as close as it was possible for her to be.

"I want the night," he told her. "The *whole* night—can I have it?"

"I want the whole night, too," she said without compunction, knowing that if she only got this one, she at least wanted all of it.

"So, a little rest," he said and nodded at the nightstand where more protection waited, "and then we put those to good use?"

"Okay," she agreed.

He kissed her forehead, his lips lingering there for several minutes before he whispered, "You're something, Abby Crane. Something so, so special."

She merely smiled, closed her eyes and said, "Just don't waste *too* much of my night with that resting stuff."

He laughed. "I promise."

Then she felt him relax around her and knew he'd drifted off.

But she didn't need to rest as much as she needed to absorb everything she could of being there in his arms like that.

So she just stayed awake, snuggled so wonderfully against him, her naked body molded perfectly to his.

And like the few things in her past that she'd been grateful to have even just once, she engraved it all into her mind, every sensation, taking solace in the fact that there was more to come.

More to come tonight, at least.

More to come of this one night she'd given herself with him.

Even if not more to come after that...

Chapter Ten

"Dylan!" Abby said, startled to find him—or anyone—sitting on the hood of her car when she left the Beauty By Design special occasions salon alone and after dark.

Lindie Camden's wedding had been ten days ago and that was the first time Abby had been face-to-face with Dylan since he'd left her apartment the following morning.

After the initial fright passed and it sank in that he was there, she had to fight the compulsion to rush to him and leap into his arms. She had to fight to keep from showing that the mere sight of him was enough to make her melt inside.

But fight she did, squaring her shoulders, raising her chin and holding her ground as she said a curt, "What are you doing here?"

He let out a disgusted half sigh and shook his head. "I'm wondering why the hell you're playing cat and mouse, why the hell I have to ambush you just to be able to see you and why the hell you won't just talk to me."

She was standing several feet away and didn't dare move any closer. All she did was shrug as if it wasn't any big deal that she'd been sneaking out the back door of the salon every time he'd come in trying to find her. That she'd left orders with everyone to say they didn't know where she was. As if it wasn't any big deal that she hadn't opened her apartment door to him any of the dozen times he'd been there knocking, or that she'd ignored his every text, every email, every message from him in her voicemail, every request through China for her to call or see him. As if it was no big deal that she'd put all her energy into not crossing paths with him in any way.

All the energy that she hadn't been expending crying and missing him.

"There's nothing to talk about," she said firmly. "You did what you set out to do—you found the lockbox, helped me know who my parents were and why I was abandoned. I'm doing the consulting work with your sisters and Jani about improving your salons—at least, we've had one meeting about it to get started. And you set the wheels into motion for buying Sheila out so Beauty By Design will be mine. You said yourself that you wanted your brother to take that over and handle it, and Derek is."

"I also told you that I wanted Derek on that so business wasn't what you and I were about. So we could be free to see where things could go between us. And you've been dodging me ever since."

There was no denying the truth so she didn't try.

"Is this because I didn't call the next day? Because the first time I did call it was just about business to see if you'd take our offer? Is it because I let a couple of days go by before I called to just talk?" he asked. "I know that was bush-league and I'm sorry for it. But I had to sort some things out—"

"It's not about phone calls. That night of the wedding was all there was ever going to be."

"What? Why?" he shouted, clearly stunned to hear that. "You can't say that night wasn't amazing!"

Again Abby merely shrugged to give the illusion that that night hadn't rocked her entire world when it had. When that night was part of the reason she'd been grieving the loss of Dylan even more than she'd grieved the loss of Mark.

But her shields were up to protect herself—protection that that night had left her all the more aware of needing *because* it had been as amazing for her as he was saying it had been for him.

"That night and how I came away from it feeling is the reason I needed to sort through things," he said, as if he thought she would change her mind if he could just explain himself.

"I came back from Europe after Lara with a plan," he told her. "First I had to make things right with my family—that was my priority. Then, when that was taken care of, I had every intention of keeping a low profile for a long time when it came to women and relationships. Lara was such a disaster. And the problems she caused just kept rippling out, spreading into everything…"

He shook his head again, and Abby stood there looking at him in the dim golden glow of the streetlight. He was wearing jeans and a hoodie. There were circles under his eyes—like there were under her concealer—that made her think he wasn't sleeping any better than she had been. And that scruff she liked so much shad-

owed a face that was even more handsome than she remembered. But for the first time, that bit of beard didn't
look like a time-of-day or a too-busy-to-shave thing. Instead she had the sense that it had come out of lack of
thought about his own appearance because he was just
too tortured to care.

But she shored herself against letting that affect her.
She'd done what she'd done because she didn't see any
other option. Regardless of whether or not it caused them
both pain. In the long run it was for the best.

"I wasn't even going to date for probably the rest
of this year and into next," he was saying. "And then
when I decided I was ready again, I was going to take
it slow with anyone I was even remotely interested in.
I was going to make sure that I got to know her so well
that there wouldn't be any surprises. No underlying issues that I didn't know about. No traps like with Lara
and that crazy-ass drive she had to stir up trouble where
there wasn't any before. I was going to make sure that
whoever I ended up with was stable and steady and
grounded. And I'll be honest with you, at first I was
convinced that that wasn't you—"

"You thought I was unstable and shaky and my head
was in the clouds?" she asked facetiously, holding on
to that admission that he'd had negative thoughts about
her. It was exactly what she'd expected, what she was
most afraid of. His confirmation validated her fears.

"No, of course I didn't think that." He slid down from
the hood of her car and stood in front of it.

His Jaguar was parked beside her compact sedan
and she wished he would just go to his own car so she
could get in hers and escape this and the effects of seeing him again.

But he continued to block her getaway. So she stayed

standing there. Wishing that she didn't have to. And at the same time grateful for every minute more of the opportunity to see him again.

"What I thought at the very beginning was that anyone who had grown up the way you had—shuffled around, without parents or a family, without discipline or with too much of the wrong kind of discipline or abused or...or who knew what—was really likely to have *issues*."

All a part of what Mark had thought.

She didn't say that. She said, "And if your spoiled rich girl had *issues,* how could I not?" More sarcasm.

"Yeah," he admitted. "But then I got to know you and everything...took off. In a flash. When I wasn't ready. When the last damn thing that was supposed to happen happened, and all of a sudden I was head over heels—more head over heels than I've ever been for anyone—*including* Lara, who I was *engaged* to. And we had that night of the wedding..." He shook his head yet again, his expression forlorn and yet still reflecting some of that amazement he'd spoken of a moment before. "That night with you was like nothing else and I really had to think about things."

"Things," she parroted.

"Things like if I'd gone off the deep end. If what I was feeling was real, and if I should try to go after what I wanted. Or if I was just obsessed or something—"

"Obsessed..." She repeated the word because in the past ten days she'd begun to wonder if she was obsessed with *him*. Why else would she be so miserable at the end of something she'd known would end? Something she'd basically ended herself? And yet "miserable" didn't even do justice to the way she'd felt these past ten days.

"Yeah, obsessed," he said. "Because I couldn't...

can't...stop thinking about you, and needing to be with you every minute. Wanting to share everything with you and have you there with me for everything—big, small, good, bad and everything in between. I can't stop thinking that I want to be there for *you* for everything, to go to bed every night and wake up every morning with you beside me. I can't stop feeling like there's just this huge hole if you aren't with me, if I'm not with you...

"But what I came to realize," he went on, "was that I hadn't gone off the deep end. That, yes, maybe I am a little obsessed, but that's only because I'm in love with you. Bad timing or not. Ready or not. Everything I'm feeling, everything I want—regardless of whether it was what I'd planned—just boils down to that. To this..."

He reached into the pouch pocket of his hoodie and took out a small velvet box that looked like a ring box.

For a moment he held it in the palm of his hand.

Abby had no idea if he meant for her to take it or not. But she knew she couldn't so she slipped her hands into the back pockets of her jeans to repress the temptation to reach out for it.

He turned just enough to set the box on the hood of her car and focused on her again.

Abby had some trouble taking her eyes off that ring box but, with a strong effort, she managed it. "Maybe you're just a sucker for unstable women," she said glibly, defensively.

"Yeah, that's the thing—the more I thought about you and everything I've come to know about you, the more I knew that regardless of how you grew up, you aren't unstable. That maybe *because* of the way you grew up, you're someone who can weather the storms and upheaval with grace—the way you did learning about your family history."

He took a step toward her and Abby stood up straighter, ready to move back if she needed to.

"The more I thought about you and everything I know about you," he continued, "The more I knew that you're someone I can trust. In every way. To look out for me, for my family, like you did with Lara at the salon that day. And, God knows, you're who I want to look out for. I realized that even though you could have come out of growing up in foster care so much differently, so much harsher, you came out of it as this really great, kind, wise person who doesn't feel entitled to even what you should feel entitled to. You're smarter than me and my whole family when it comes to seeing through people like Lara. And you're somebody who has your feet firmly planted and your head *not* in the clouds..."

He sighed, shook his head once more and said, "The worst thing I can say about you is what I've been butting my head up against for the last week. The underlying issue you *do* have is this—" He made a frustrated gesture with one arm that shot up into the air before he put both his hands in the hoodie's kangaroo pocket.

Those hands that she remembered the touch of too, too well...

"I know what you're doing here, Abby," he said solemnly. "I know you've gone into self-preservation mode. Whether because I didn't call the way I should have or—"

"It isn't because you didn't call," she reiterated.

"Then what the hell is it?" he demanded, his voice louder. "Tell me so I can fix it."

"So you can fix me?" she asked with more snideness, more challenge. The word reminded her why things couldn't work between them and triggered more strength to deny herself and him—despite all the good

things he'd said about her and the fact that he'd told her
he loved her.

Which was making this all the more difficult. Because, yes, her feelings for him were even deeper than
what she'd believed was love for Mark.

"So I can fix the *problem*, not you," Dylan insisted.
"With everything I've just said to you, how can you
believe that I think *anything* about you needs fixing?"

"Maybe not right now," she said. "But down the road?
I'm not up to Camden standards and never will be." It
was the phrase he'd used about Camden Superstores'
salons and the people working in them. But she thought
it applied to her, too.

"Camden standards?" he echoed with disbelief.

"I overheard you and Cade that Sunday when China
and I were at your grandmother's house for dinner," she
said. "I didn't mean to, but I did. I heard him warning
you to keep it cool with me. I heard you tell him I'm a
fish out of water with you all—"

"Whoa! I remember that conversation with Cade. In
the first place, what he was saying wasn't about you,
it was about me. He could see that I liked you and he
thought I needed to keep it cool because I'd been so
clueless when it came to Lara and I needed to regroup
before I started anything up with anyone else. And what
I said—if I recall—was *not* that you were a fish out of
water with us, but that I was sticking close to you because I didn't want you to *feel* like a fish out of water—
which was what *you* were afraid of, if memory serves."

"Which neither of us would have had to think about
if I was someone else," she countered. "Look, you've
been great to me. Your whole family has been. And I
appreciate everything you've done, everything you're
doing. But when it comes to things between us..." She

had to swallow to keep her voice from weakening and giving away just how much it hurt to say this. "When it comes to things between us, this can't go anywhere. Even if you think it would be okay, take it from me, it wouldn't be."

"Because some pretentious jerk didn't think you were good enough for him?"

"Because I'm just…who and what I am. Because I'm not the daughter of the owner of a bunch of banks—"

"The daughter of the owner of a bunch of banks put me through hell."

"Because I didn't grow up in a way that you can relate to," she went on, ignoring his comment. "A way that doesn't freak you out on some level. And don't say it doesn't, because I've seen it—"

"It doesn't freak me out. It makes me sad but—"

"And that makes you feel sorry for me and I don't want your pity, either."

Because there had been some of that from Mark, too, as well as from too many teachers or bleeding hearts or do-gooders over the years, and it somehow always made her feel less than she was.

"You and I wouldn't be okay together in the long run because I didn't go to private schools. Or college. Because I'm just a worker bee and you're…a *Camden*. Because I'm not comfortable even visiting places like where you live. Because I don't fit—"

"I'll sell the damn loft and move in with you if that's what you want! And I don't give a damn about any of that other stuff, Abby!"

But he would. He would come to after a while. It would creep up on them the same way it had with Mark. When something happened that she wasn't equipped for or educated enough to deal with, when one day he looked at her and saw that she wasn't what he'd always assumed he would end up with—his own kind.

And she would feel the way she had as a kid in situations she hadn't been cut out for—embarrassed and humiliated and as if some kind of spotlight was shining on her insufficiencies.

And Dylan would be just as embarrassed as Mark had been. And ashamed. And disappointed.

And sad.

And he *would* pity her for her shortcomings somewhere in that, too.

But he would also probably feel too guilty to just walk away, thanks to the part his family had played in her circumstances.

And none of that added up to a happy future, a happy life together.

She knew it. She felt it as surely as she felt the night air on her skin.

But she didn't say any of it because she also knew that he would just deny it.

Instead, the reason she added on to what she'd already said was, "It can't work between us because I'm the kind of person who *doesn't* want to be a Camden executive, and the same way I knew I couldn't be that, I know I couldn't be a Camden."

And she knew how much it hurt when she tried to be more than what she was, when she tried to be what someone else expected and wanted her to be, and came up short.

Plus, this was Dylan. Dylan, whom she would rather cut off her right arm than embarrass or disappointment.

Whose beautiful blue eyes she couldn't bear the thought of looking into and seeing shame or pity or guilt.

This was Dylan, who came complete with her idea

of the perfect family. A family who might have been kind to her and to China and to the rest of the special occasions team, who might be grateful for what they'd all done for the wedding. But who would eventually look at her and only be able to think that she was nothing more than the daughter of a thug they'd used to do their dirty work.

She would come to be nothing but a reminder of something ugly that they wanted to distance themselves from. She'd become some*one* they'd wish they could distance themselves from.

And how horrible would it feel when it came to that? After knowing for any amount of time at all what it was really like to be a part of that perfect family she'd always dreamed of...

"I don't know what you think it means to *be* a Camden," Dylan said, breaking into her thoughts, sounding frustrated. "And I don't care. I only care about having what we've had together and continuing to have it under any circumstances."

It was her turn to shake her head. "You say that now. But when time went on and I couldn't live up to—"

"Don't say my *standards*! You're a million times better than what my *standards* have been—I told you that."

"You couldn't believe or understand that I didn't want to be a Camden executive. To you that was unthinkable. And probably dumb and shortsighted and silly. And that's only the beginning, Dylan. I know my limitations—"

"You don't have any limitations!"

"Everybody has limitations. I just know better than most people where mine are. Where my place is in the world. And my place isn't as a *Camden*. Eventually you and the rest of your family would see it. Know it. And

be sorry for it the same way you were sorry for not seeing what your former fiancée really was. And in the
meantime I would have been trying to be what I'm not,
trying to please you and your family, and—"

"It just wouldn't be that way, Abby," he shouted.
"That isn't who *we* are. Nothing matters to me, to any
of us, except the kind of person you are. The kind of
person who goes the extra mile to help us out for a wedding even without the time to pull it off. The kind of
person who doesn't feed into mudslinging but cuts it
off at the pass. The kind of person…hell. The kind of
person you *are*!"

But it wouldn't be enough and whether or not he saw
that now, she did.

So once more she shook her head, but this time with
far, far more finality than anything that had come before.

Then she nodded at the ring box on the hood of her
car and said, "Take that back. We just don't have a future."

Don't cry. Don't cry. Don't cry…

"I'm in love with you, dammit!" he shouted again.
"And I know you aren't as stony as you're pretending to
be right now. I know what we've had. I know what we
had that night. Don't let other things stand between us."

"Things are the way they are," she said firmly. But
why did her voice have to come out so softly? Why did
it have to crack and make her sound so defeated?

"They don't have to be that way if you don't let them."

"Yeah, they do," she barely whispered.

Then she went around him to the driver's door of her
car and opened it.

Dylan was still standing there in front of the sedan,
his back to her now, shaking his head again.

Even though he couldn't see her she nodded at the velvet box on her car again and said, "Take that with you."

But he didn't. He just walked away without saying another word, leaving it there as he got into his Jaguar and sat behind the wheel, his expression one of complete disbelief.

Abby didn't know what else to do. She couldn't drive off with that ring box on her car.

So she went to it and picked it up.

Oh, God...

She held on so tight to it.

She wanted to open it. To see the ring.

She wanted to put it on her finger. To say yes.

And heaven help her, nothing she did could stop the tears from welling up in her eyes. From falling down her cheeks.

But pretending that they weren't there, she took that ring box around to his car.

And set it on the hood because she couldn't take it to his window and let him see that she was crying.

Then she returned to her own car, got in and started the engine.

Driving away from the one man in the world who made her wish she and everything else could be different.

Chapter Eleven

"*I'm telling you, Ab, I think you're wrong about everything. You're wrecking a good thing and ripping out your own heart when you don't have to.*"

China was nothing if not blunt and that's just what she'd been while she was in Abby's apartment.

Abby knew that she'd pushed her friend's patience to the limit and she didn't blame China. For some reason, even when she'd mourned the breakup with Mark, she'd managed to be somewhat more stoic about it.

But with Dylan? She was a soggy, weepy, whining, feeling-sorry-for-herself mess and she just couldn't seem to get herself out of it. In fact, she'd only gotten worse after seeing him on Tuesday night.

Everything he'd said replayed itself over and over in her mind around the clock. She couldn't sleep. She couldn't eat. She couldn't stop thinking about him. And about that ring. And she was a wreck!

Now it was Friday evening. China had come over to

check on her before going out. After finding her in yet another puddle of tears, Abby's best friend had reached her limit.

China had read her the riot act.

"I'm going out on a blind date set up for me by two of the Camdens. The date is with the son of one of their richy-rich friends. If they had any problems with you or me, with how we grew up or who we are, would they do that?" China had demanded.

"There hasn't been a single minute I've spent with those people when I felt like they thought I was any-thing less than they are," she'd gone on. *"Neither of us could say that about Mark. Look at this the way it re-ally is and not under the doom and gloom of anything from the past. Dylan's grandmother's best friends are people who started out as her maid and her gardener. Now those people are part of the family. A whole huge family with all kinds of people in it!"* China had railed.

"You want this guy," she'd said without question. *"More than I think you've ever wanted any guy. So quit thinking so much, use that cold pack I gave you for your face to get all that puffiness out, put on some makeup, go find Dylan and say yes, for cripes' sake! Be happy and forget the rest!"*

And out China had gone to meet her blind date. Without the slightest indication of hesitancy or concern that worlds might collide if she and her date ended up to-gether.

And there Abby was, sitting alone in her apartment. In the fading light of day. Without so much as a lamp on. Drowning in her own misery.

How dumb was that? she asked herself.

It seemed pretty dumb.

But, at the same time, she knew that everything that

had led her to reject Dylan wasn't just in her imagination. There were valid reasons for concern.

Except that as she thought about it and replayed China's words, she began to wonder if there was some middle ground between China's choice—to act as though those concerns didn't exist, and the choice Abby had made up to now—to believe that those concerns overshadowed everything else.

After all, the Camdens *were* still the Camdens—one of Colorado's most preeminent families and she was still the daughter of their former strong-arm enforcer who had grown up without a drop of privilege or culture and without the education they had.

And she was all too familiar with what happened with wide gaps like that between two people trying to have a future together.

Yes, Mark had been kind of rigid and pretentious and overly concerned with appearances, and that wasn't Dylan. But being a Camden still came with expectations and obligations—she'd done enough high-society weddings and special events to see for herself what went along with his kind of status. She'd overheard enough judgmental conversations to know what was said of someone marrying *beneath* them—*socially slumming.* And she didn't want to be out of her depth with another man. Even more out of her depth than she'd been with Mark.

It did occur to her, though, that what she was worried about was being out of her depth in his world. When it came to Dylan himself, she'd never felt out of her depth.

Even at his loft, when she'd felt uncomfortable in those surroundings, she'd still felt comfortable with him.

They just clicked so well…

So did she really mind if snobby people talked or looked down on his having a connection with her?

She wouldn't be bothered by it, she decided. She just didn't want *him* to care. The way Mark had.

But would Dylan care?

He'd said he didn't, wouldn't. And China was right about his family embracing Margaret and Louie—Dylan had done that, too. It was something she'd lost sight of when she'd been thinking about it before.

It didn't seem to matter to him or to any of the Camdens that two people who worked for them had also had large roles in raising the Camden grandchildren. Instead the Haliburtons were included the way any aunt and uncle would be. The way the Camdens had included her and China at their Sunday dinner, had included her in the rehearsal festivities, and her and her entire team in the wedding.

China was right, too, that the Camden family was a huge group with all kinds of people also accepted into it—something else that Abby hadn't taken into consideration before.

All kinds of people with different backgrounds and interests. And all of that was embraced by the Camdens. Celebrated, even. She hadn't seen anything that made her think any of the additions to the Camden family had been asked or expected to change. Not even Sawyer Huffman—Lindie's groom—who was and would continue to be the Camdens' business adversary. If Dylan hadn't told her about all of that she would never have guessed, because Sawyer was treated and included the same way everyone else was.

The whole family was just so…regular. There wasn't even anything about GiGi herself that was lofty or snooty or snobby—she and Margaret and Abby had sat together at the rehearsal dinner party playing blackjack like three friends.

So maybe China was right—the Camdens hadn't given any indication that they thought any less of her or her friend. And with the explanation Dylan had given, it was easier to believe that what she'd overheard Cade say to Dylan that Sunday really hadn't been about her not being good enough for him.

But there had also been Dylan's job offer...

Everything that had come along with that had reminded her of Mark—there had been so many things that Mark had wanted to change about her to make her fit into that slot.

But when she thought about it now, she realized that Dylan hadn't proposed covering up anything about her history or her, he hadn't wanted to make up a shinier backstory for her. Dylan had genuinely only been trying to make things easier and more comfortable for her.

More important, not only had he accepted her rejection of that offer, he'd reassessed, listened to things she'd told him, and come up with an offer that—to Abby—was so much better. An offer that was in line with what she was not only capable of, but something that was a dream come true—owning a shop of her own. Two shops and the special occasions location, actually.

And he'd done that without attempting to change a thing about her. In fact, he had enough respect for her and her knowledge of salons to hire her to counsel his sisters and cousin on Camden Superstores salons.

She'd been with Mark the entire time she'd helped redesign and remodel both locations for Beauty By Design and he'd shrugged it off and reduced it to what he'd called her *little work project*.

But once Dylan had accepted that she didn't want to

be a Camden executive, he'd gone on to treat her owning two simple beauty salons and a shop for special events work as every bit as important as any position he could offer her. Which it was to her.

So maybe she should start trusting him and the things he'd said to her. Instead of doubting him because her trust in Mark had been so unfounded.

And maybe she should put a cold pack on her face…

She went to her freezer and took a facemask out, taking it with her to plop down into her sole easy chair and resting her head back to fit the icy pack over her sore and swollen eyes and cheeks.

The mask had slots to see through, and what was directly in her line of vision from there was her bed.

She hadn't slept in it since the night she'd shared it with Dylan.

Even when she'd tried to sleep, it had been either on her couch or on China's.

Because Dylan was right—their night together in that bed had been so amazing it had made it impossible for her to go back to it, believing that she would never again be in it *with* him. It had turned her bed into a bed of nails.

So what are you doing here, Ab? she asked herself, the voice in her head more China's than her own.

She loved Dylan. She knew that. She'd come to accept it after seeing him again Tuesday night. After what he'd said. After wanting so badly to look at that ring. To put it on her finger. To let it seal her to him.

Maybe that's why she'd been so inconsolable since then.

Because she did love him. With all her heart.

And what if he honestly didn't care that she was who she was or where she'd come from? What if he didn't think she needed to be fixed or changed or upgraded? What if there was also the chance that his family could accept her and that she could be a part of that perfect, dream family?

Then why *was* she thinking so much? Why didn't she just say yes and be happy?

Since Mark she hadn't been too sure that happily-ever-after was really possible for her. But maybe—like China had said—she was wrong…

Or maybe the ice pack was just freezing her brain…

Or numbing it enough to get it out of the way of her heart telling her what she really should do.

And her heart was telling her to go after Dylan.

And let herself have what she wanted.

And be happy.

She wasn't sure how long she was supposed to sit with the ice pack on.

But she also couldn't waste another minute sitting there and not going after Dylan.

So she took the mask off and rushed to her bathroom to do what damage control she could with makeup, taking her hair out of the rubber band that held it contained and brushing it into its naturally wild curls.

Then she tore off the pajama pants and top she'd already put on for the night and replaced them with jeans, a lacy tank top and an off-the-shoulder navy blue T-shirt that left the tank top's bra-like straps showing with a sexy allure.

Because she might need a little ammunition.

She just hoped that some shoulder action was enough…

Dylan had been mad at her Tuesday night. Frustrated and hurt and angry.

And she doubted that that had gotten better since then.

In fact, it might have gotten worse.

He might have crossed the line between anger and hurt and frustration to hating her and not wanting anything to do with her.

Oh, how horrible would *that* be if it was true?

But she couldn't think about that, either. If she did, she was never going to get out of her apartment door.

So she pushed the thoughts aside, picked up her purse and car keys and headed out.

Just hoping she wasn't too late…

Boy, did she hate where Dylan lived!

Abby hated it so much that after finding parking and being forced to tell a doorman through a speaker who it was she wanted to see and waiting for the doorman to apparently call up to Dylan's loft for permission to let her in, she had second thoughts as she walked across the lobby to the three private elevators.

But then she reached the elevator bank and discovered that the doors to Dylan's were already open.

He'd told her that he did that from his loft to let guests come up. Which meant that not only had he given permission to let her into the building, he was giving her access to him.

So those open elevator doors looked a little like open arms to her.

But then she stepped into the elevator and got nervous all over again when it started to rise. It struck her that she didn't know what she was going to say when those elevator doors opened again.

Dylan was standing in front of them when they did. He looked much the way he had Tuesday night—shadows under his eyes, scruff on that face she just wanted to reach out and touch.

He was wearing jeans and a plain gray short-sleeved crewneck T-shirt that reassured her that he was not entertaining anyone. She was relieved that even in his posh surroundings he looked like someone she could relate to.

But she still didn't know what to say and there he was.

"Hi," was all she could come up with.

"Hi," he said in a voice that sounded craggy and worn, and made her think once again that he was in bad shape, too.

"I guess it's your turn to ask what I'm doing here," she said softly.

"Guess it is."

So much for feeling like those open elevator doors were welcoming open arms. Because that was not what she was being met with. Instead his arms were crossed over his chest, as if he was protecting himself from her.

"Would you like it better if I wasn't here at all?" she asked, remembering that that was how she'd felt on Tuesday night.

He shook his head and sighed. Then he said, "No. Come in."

He turned his back to her, freeing the way and giving her a view of what she thought was the best derriere in the world. But still, it wasn't a warm invitation.

She left the elevator, hesitating to follow him but deciding there was nothing else for her to do. She trailed behind him into the living room portion of his loft, reaching it just as he turned to face her again, propping one hip on the corner edge of his sofa and staring at her. Waiting for her, she assumed, to tell him what she was doing there.

So she did. She just didn't know what else to do but lay her heart out the same way he had on Tuesday night, telling him all she'd thought about after China had lit into her and left earlier.

"I'm sorry, Dylan," she concluded when she'd completely opened herself up to him. "It's just that you're... you. And I'm just the foster kid people get freaked out about because of their own weird ideas. And..." She shrugged. "I don't know. I thought that mattered."

"It doesn't," he said firmly. "Not to me. Not to my family."

"Not now. But what about later?" she just had to ask. "Later, when it might come up with someone that I was abandoned in a hospital waiting room when I was two and grew up in thirty-some different homes without parents of my own? Or if it should come up that I didn't know either of my parents or even who they were until after they were dead, when my father died in prison for killing a man? What happens when I have to say no, I never went to college, I was lucky to graduate high school? That in my whole life I've never traveled out of the state or—"

"If I ever run into anyone who hears or knows any of that and can't handle it, then they're people I don't ever need to run into again. They're not people I want or need in my life. And certainly not in place of you."

It was the first sign he'd given her that maybe he hadn't crossed that line into hating her.

Then it finally got better because he said, "I want you, Abby. Just you. I don't care about the rest. I told you where I stand on that."

"But are you sure..."

He dropped his head back and shook it in frustration before he drew it upright again to scowl at her and said facetiously, "No, I'm not sure. I went out and bought a ring and asked you to marry me but I still have my doubts."

Abby smiled sheepishly. "Did you take the ring back to the store?"

"No, I don't give up that easily. I was going to talk to China next to see if I could get her to talk some sense into you."

"Good plan but she did it on her own tonight." Then something else occurred to her. "Is it the ring you bought for that crazy woman?"

He laughed again and once more shook his head at her. "The crazy woman had a family heirloom ring, so no, your ring is just your ring."

"Is it mine?"

"Not until you damn well say yes!"

"You never actually asked. You just sort of said it was what you wanted," she pointed out.

He pushed off of the sofa and disappeared into his bedroom. When he came back he had the ring box in his fist. He brought it with him to stand in front of her.

"Do you want me on one knee? Or both?"

She wrinkled her nose and shook her head, not liking the idea of having this man of all men on his knees to her. "No."

He stayed standing but he didn't give her the ring box. He kept hold of it, tipped her chin up with the crooked index finger of his other hand so he could look into her eyes, and said, "I'm in love with you, Abby-of-the-crane-blanket. I want you to marry me. I want you to be my wife. I want you to come and be a part of my family. I want us to make a family of our own and let that be the family you didn't have before. I just want you to be mine...now and forever..."

Tears swelled in her eyes once more but this time

they were only from that happiness that was finally right there in front of her for the taking.

"That's what I want, too. All of it. But mostly just you," she whispered around the lump in her throat.

He sighed in relief then and wrapped her in his arms, pulling her to him tightly enough to let her know that holding her like that was something he'd ached for and needed.

But it was what she'd ached for and needed, too, so she just melted into him, curling her own arms around him and resting her cheek to his chest.

They stayed that way for a few minutes before he again raised her chin to kiss her, a long, deep kiss that reclaimed all they'd almost lost.

Only then did he let go of her with one arm and bring the hand with the ring box in it back around, opening his fist to offer it to her from his palm.

With her pulse racing, Abby took the velvet box they'd volleyed on Tuesday night and opened it.

Inside was a platinum engagement ring with a diamond bigger than any she'd ever seen on any bride she'd worked for.

"Oh, dear…" she said, flabbergasted by it. "It's gigantic…"

But Dylan didn't pay any attention to that.

He took the ring out of the box, reached for her left hand and put it on her.

"That's it," he said definitively. "It's a done deal. You can't back out now."

"Well, just because it's such a pretty ring," she joked.

But the truth was that the ring—no matter how beautiful—surprisingly didn't really make any difference to her. Yes, it was like one of her and China's fantasies coming to life. But now as she looked at it she realized that no fantasy compared to what that ring actually meant.

Because what it meant was that Dylan truly loved her. That he truly wanted her. That he was truly committed to having a life with her, a future.

It meant that she could trust that she was going to have this man she loved more than she'd ever imagined possible. And nothing mattered more than that.

So when that man pulled her back into his arms, into another of those kisses that she'd been starved for for nearly two weeks, she knew that regardless of where they were or where they'd come from, his arms would be home for her from that moment on.

That he would be the family she'd never had.

And that not only were there really happily-ever-afters, but there, with him, she'd found hers.

* * * * *

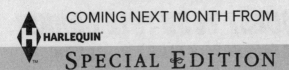
Available January 19, 2016

#2455 FORTUNE'S PERFECT VALENTINE
The Fortunes of Texas: All Fortune's Children • by Stella Bagwell
Computer programmer Vivian Blair believes the secret to a successful marriage is
compatibility, while her boss, Wes Robinson, thinks passion's the only ingredient in
a romance. When she develops a matchmaking app and challenges him to use it,
which one will prove the other right...and find true love?

#2456 DR. FORGET-ME-NOT
Matchmaking Mamas • by Marie Ferrarella
When Dr. Mitchell Stewart begins volunteering at a shelter alongside teacher
Melanie McAdams, he falls head-over-stethoscope for the blonde beauty. Once
burned in love, Melanie's not looking for forever, even in the capable arms of a man
like Mitchell. Can the medic's bedside manner convince Melanie to open her heart
to a happy ending?

#2457 A SOLDIER'S PROMISE
Wed in the West • by Karen Templeton
Former soldier Levi Talbot returns to Whispering Pines, New Mexico, to make
good on his promise to look after his best friend's family. The last thing he expects
is to fall in love with his pal's widow, Valerie Lopez. Now, Levi's in for the battle of
his life—one he's determined to win.

#2458 THE DOCTOR'S VALENTINE DARE
Rx for Love • by Cindy Kirk
Dr. Noah Anson's can-do attitude has always met with success, both
professionally and personally. But when he runs up against the most stubborn
woman in Jackson Hole, Josie Campbell, nothing goes the way he planned. It
will take a whole lotta lovin' to win Josie's heart...and that's what he's
determined to do!

#2459 WAKING UP WED
Sugar Falls, Idaho • by Christy Jeffries
When old friends Kylie Chatterson and Drew Gregson wake up in Las Vegas with
matching wedding bands, all they want to say is "I don't!" But when they're forced
to live together and care for Drew's twin nephews, they realize married life might
be the happy ending they'd both always dreamed of.

#2460 A VALENTINE FOR THE VETERINARIAN
Paradise Animal Clinic • by Katie Meyer
Single mom and veterinarian Cassie Marshall swore off men for good when her ex
walked out on her. But Alex Santiago, new to Paradise and its police department,
and his adorable K9 partner melt Cassie's heart. This Valentine's Day, can the doc
and the deputy create a forever family?

**YOU CAN FIND MORE INFORMATION ON UPCOMING HARLEQUIN® TITLES,
FREE EXCERPTS AND MORE AT WWW.HARLEQUIN.COM.**

HSECNM0116

REQUEST YOUR FREE BOOKS!
2 FREE NOVELS PLUS 2 FREE GIFTS!

⧫ HARLEQUIN®

SPECIAL EDITION
Life, Love & Family

YES! Please send me 2 FREE Harlequin® Special Edition novels and my 2 FREE gifts (gifts are worth about $10). After receiving them, if I don't wish to receive any more books, I can return the shipping statement marked "cancel." If I don't cancel, I will receive 6 brand-new novels every month and be billed just $4.74 per book in the U.S. or $5.49 per book in Canada. That's a savings of at least 12% off the cover price! It's quite a bargain! Shipping and handling is just 50¢ per book in the U.S. and 75¢ per book in Canada.* I understand that accepting the 2 free books and gifts places me under no obligation to buy anything. I can always return a shipment and cancel at any time. Even if I never buy another book, the two free books and gifts are mine to keep forever.

235/335 HDN GH3Z

Name	(PLEASE PRINT)	

Address		Apt. #

City	State/Prov.	Zip/Postal Code

Signature (if under 18, a parent or guardian must sign)

Mail to the **Reader Service:**
IN U.S.A.: P.O. Box 1867, Buffalo, NY 14240-1867
IN CANADA: P.O. Box 609, Fort Erie, Ontario L2A 5X3

Want to try two free books from another line?
Call 1-800-873-8635 or visit www.ReaderService.com.

* Terms and prices subject to change without notice. Prices do not include applicable taxes. Sales tax applicable in N.Y. Canadian residents will be charged applicable taxes. Offer not valid in Quebec. This offer is limited to one order per household. Not valid for current subscribers to Harlequin Special Edition books. All orders subject to credit approval. Credit or debit balances in a customer's account(s) may be offset by any other outstanding balance owed by or to the customer. Please allow 4 to 6 weeks for delivery. Offer available while quantities last.

Your Privacy—The Reader Service is committed to protecting your privacy. Our Privacy Policy is available online at www.ReaderService.com or upon request from the Reader Service.

We make a portion of our mailing list available to reputable third parties that offer products we believe may interest you. If you prefer that we not exchange your name with third parties, or if you wish to clarify or modify your communication preferences, please visit us at www.ReaderService.com/consumerchoice or write to us at Reader Service Preference Service, P.O. Box 9062, Buffalo, NY 14240-9062. Include your complete name and address.

HSE15

Closing her eyes for a moment, Melanie sighed. She had no answer for the taunting voice in her head. No theory to put forth to satisfy her conscience and this sudden, unannounced huge wave of guilt that had just washed over her like a tsunami after a 9.9 earthquake. And, like it or not, that was what Mitch's kiss had felt like to her, an earthquake. A great, big, giant earthquake and she wasn't even sure if the ground beneath her feet hadn't disappeared altogether, thanks to liquefaction. She felt just that unsteady.

She'd stayed sitting down even after Mitch had left the room.

Damn it, the man kissed you. He didn't perform a lobotomy on you with his tongue. Get a grip and get back to work. Life goes on, remember?

That was just the problem. Life went on. The love of her life had been taken away ten months ago and for some reason, life still went on.

Squaring her shoulders, she slid off the makeshift exam table, otherwise known in her mind as the scene of the crime, tested the steadiness of her legs and, once that was established, left the room.

Whether Melanie liked it or not, there was still a lot of work to do, and it wasn't going to get done by itself.

She had almost managed to talk herself into a neutral, rational place as she made her way past the dining hall, which, when Mitch was here, still served as his unofficial waiting room. That was when she heard Mitch call out to her.

"Melanie, I need you."

Everything inside her completely froze.

It was the same outside. It was as if her legs, after working fine all these years, had suddenly forgotten how to move and take her from point A to point B.

She had to have heard him wrong.

The Dr. Mitchell Stewart she had come to know these past few weeks would have never uttered those words to anyone, least of all to her.

And would the Mitchell Stewart you think you know so well have singed off your lips like that?

Don't miss
DR. FORGET-ME-NOT
by USA TODAY *bestselling author Marie Ferrarella,*
available February 2016 wherever
Harlequin® Special Edition books and ebooks are sold.

www.Harlequin.com

Turn your love of reading into rewards you'll love with

Harlequin My Rewards

**Join for FREE today at
www.HarlequinMyRewards.com**

Earn **FREE BOOKS** of your choice.

Experience **EXCLUSIVE OFFERS** and contests.

Enjoy **BOOK RECOMMENDATIONS**
selected just for you.

PLUS! Sign up now
and get **500** points
right away!

Earn **FREE** REWARDS
HarlequinMyRewards.com
Join Today!

MYR16R

Love the Harlequin book you just read?

Your opinion matters.

Review this book on your favorite book site, review site, blog or your own social media properties and share your opinion with other readers!

Be sure to connect with us at:
Harlequin.com/Newsletters
Facebook.com/HarlequinBooks
Twitter.com/HarlequinBooks